Q0063 73287

D0785080

This
be
date

Do You Speak Chocolate?

Do You Speak Chocolate?

Cas Lester

Piccadilly
PRESS

First published in Great Britain in 2017 by
PICCADILLY PRESS
80–81 Wimpole St, London W1G 9RE
www.piccadillypress.co.uk

Text copyright © Cas Lester, 2017
Illustrations copyright © Kate Forrester

All rights reserved.
No part of this publication may be reproduced, stored or transmitted in
any form by any means, electronic, mechanical, photocopying or
otherwise, without the prior written permission of the publisher.

The right of Cas Lester and Kate Forrester to be identified as author and
illustrator of this work has been asserted by them in accordance with the
Copyright, Designs and Patents Act, 1988

This is a work of fiction. Names, places, events and incidents are either
the products of the authors imagination or used fictitiously. Any
resemblance to actual persons, living or dead, is purely coincidental.

A CIP catalogue record for this book is available from the British Library.

ISBN: 978-1-47140-503-7
also available as an ebook

2

Typeset in Sabon by
Palimpsest Book Production Ltd, Falkirk, Stirlingshire

Printed and bound in Great Britain by Clays Ltd, St Ives plc

Piccadilly Press is an imprint of Bonnier Zaffre Ltd,
a Bonnier Publishing company
www.bonnierpublishing.com

*For my friends,
with loads of love,
to thank you
for everything.*

1
Skirts!

I can remember *exactly* the day I met Nadima. It was the day I got my three big brothers to wear skirts to school. Yes, seriously.

It was summer, and boiling hot, and everyone was sweating away in long black trousers. So I'd started this petition to wear shorts and I wanted to get the *entire* school to sign it. I was launching the campaign by wearing my PE shorts to school, so I asked my mate Lily if she'd wear hers too and she said yes. Then she went and told her mate Kara, and Kara told her not to because she'd get into trouble. So the night before, *right at the very last minute*, Lily texted me.

Sorry Jaz. Not wearing shorts to school. Lil x

*

Seriously? Thanks a bundle, Lil. It wasn't like her to do that to me, but I might have guessed Kara would stick her big nose in.

So then I'd had the *brilliant* idea of getting The Brothers to wear *skirts*!

They thought it'd be a laugh. Me too. Well, it seemed like a good idea – at the time.

That morning, as we all piled out of Mum's car at school, *everyone* was pointing and laughing. To be fair, The Brothers looked *hilarious*! Miniskirts are *so* not the right fashion statement for *any* of them – they just don't have the legs! Or the shoes!

'I want to die, *now*,' moaned Dan, tugging at his skirt.

'I am going straight to the toilets to change,' announced Gus.

Technically Gus is the youngest Big Bro – but he's going to be the biggest. He's only in Year 9 but he's as tall as Dan already, and Dan's in Year 11. Matt's my oldest Big Bro – he's in the sixth form. He stood glaring at me in the drop-off area and muttered, 'I look ridiculous.'

He was right. He's six foot two, and his skirt barely covered his boxers.

'Man up, Big Bro!' I laughed, slapping him on

the back. Then we trooped into school – and walked slap bang straight into the head teacher.

Mrs C instantly launched into us for 'not wearing school uniform'.

'Yes, we are!' I argued. 'These are my PE shorts and those are school skirts!'

'School uniform for boys is trousers, not skirts,' she replied.

'Does it actually say that boys can't wear skirts?' I challenged.

'Well, no,' she admitted. 'Not as such.'

'Well then!' I retorted. She gave me a look over the top of her glasses.

'Jaz Watson, I've lost count of the number of times you've broken the school rules, and you're only in Year 7. Are you trying to get in the *Guinness Book of Records* or something?'

'No, miss! And anyway, I only break the stupid ones.'

Mrs C raised an eyebrow. Matt gave me a nudge and Gus trod on my foot.

'You're heading for an after-school detention,' warned Mrs C.

There was a sharp intake of breath from The Brothers.

'Seriously, miss?' I protested.

'Yes, seriously,' she replied. Then she made us change into ordinary uniform – from the lost-property box. I ended up in a skanky pair of trousers about six inches too short. They looked gross, smelled worse and I looked totally stupid in them.

As soon as I walked into our form room Kara snorted with laughter.

'*What* are you wearing?'

So then of course everyone stared at me.

'A ballgown,' I replied, sarcastically – which got a huge laugh from everyone except Kara.

'But I thought you were going to wear your shorts?' she said, trying to look all innocent.

'I did. Mrs C made me change.'

Kara turned to Lily. 'I told you she'd get into trouble.'

Lily grimaced. They were both sitting on their table, with Chloe and Elly.

'As a matter of fact, I didn't get into trouble,' I said, *sort of* truthfully.

(I didn't mention that Mrs C had threatened me with a detention. And anyhow, I didn't care. It was for a good cause.)

Sliding into my seat at the next table, I dumped

my bag on the floor. 'Actually, Mrs C asked if I was trying to get into the *Guinness Book of Records*.'

'Are you?' gasped Chloe. 'That'd be so cool!'

Honestly, Chloe would believe anything.

'No, you muppet!' I laughed.

'So why *were* you wearing shorts?' asked Elly.

'She's launching a petition so everyone can wear them,' explained Lily.

'Awesome!' said Ryan. 'I'd sign that.'

'Me too,' nodded Liam. Ryan and Liam are the class clowns and they sit on my table – which is a good laugh. I got out the petition and they signed it. Wow, I thought, two whole signatures.

'I wasn't meant to be the *only* one wearing shorts,' I said, looking directly at Lily.

Her face fell, which was fine by me.

'Don't give Lily a hard time!' snapped Kara. 'You can't expect everyone to do what you want.'

Which was pretty rich coming from her, and I was just about to say so, but then Mrs W, our form teacher, came in.

Kara spent most of registration whispering to Lily and flicking me sharp little looks – so I guessed she was talking about me.

Oh, how absolutely great.

2
❦ English ❧

After registration it was double English. I hate English. And I double hate double English.

Mum tells me to think of English as 'a challenge I can overcome with my fabulous ability to tackle any obstacle'. Now, I would happily think of English as 'a challenge I can overcome with my fabulous ability to tackle any obstacle' if I didn't have a *dorkbrain* for a teacher. Mr Y seems to think English lessons should be slow death by humiliation.

He *always* picks one of the dyslexic kids to read *out loud* to the rest of the class. And it's usually me. Why?! WHY?! I'm *spectacularly* dyslexic. And anyhow, there are *loads* of kids who love reading out loud – all those drama wannabes for a start. (Kara, for one.) So why pick on me?

Or he'll ask the whole class a question and then choose me to answer it, *even when I haven't got my hand up*. Why not ask one of the kids waggling their hands frantically in the air, who obviously *do* know the answer? What is the point of asking someone who clearly *doesn't*?

Seriously, the man's an idiot.

I sat there, bracing myself for the usual crushing, as Mr Y handed back our homework. I flipped open my book. As usual, it was *plastered* with bright red crosses, squiggly underlinings and sad faces.

Honestly, there ought to be a law banning teachers from using emojis. It's *sooo* embarrassing when they try to be trendy. AND he'd put 'check your spelling' in large letters at the bottom. How can I *check my spelling* if I don't know how things are spelt in the first place?

Yup, like I said, the man's an idiot.

Anyhow, I couldn't give a bouncing banana about spelling, because:

a) all computers have spellcheck
b) the spelling rules in the English language are

STUPID. How can 'road' be spelt 'r-o-d-e' and 'r-o-w-e-d' *as well*?

c) making spelling mistakes can be a good thing. I happen to know that artificial sweeteners were invented when someone wrote 'taste' the results instead of 'test' the results in a scientific experiment. So if someone hadn't made a spelling mistake, that brilliant scientific discovery would never have been made and the world wouldn't have Diet Coke.

By now Mr Y was handing out worksheets. 'Today we're working on Persuasive Writing Skills. Any good piece of Persuasive Writing should make at least three good arguments,' he announced.

Why three? I thought. Why can't you have just one really good one? And, btw, who says so?

Mr Y was still talking. 'I want you to come up with three reasons why you should pick your own bedtime, put them down as bullet points, and then write a short summary of your arguments at the bottom.'

I was struggling to follow him. Partly because I'm not great when I'm given lots of instructions all at once, but *mostly* because I'd zoned out. I was worrying about being mean to Lily earlier. So, as soon as Mr Y's back was turned, I ripped a bit out of my exercise book and wrote her a note.

Lil Im sory Jx

I leaned over to hand it to her, but just as she took it Mr Y looked round.

'Jaz Watson!' he snapped. 'Get on with your work! You, of all people in this class, need to work harder in English. And stop distracting other people who . . .' He was just about to go off on one about how crucial English is to *all* of our futures (yawn, yawn) when the classroom door opened and we were saved by Mrs C. She was bringing in a girl wearing our school uniform and a matching blue headscarf.

3

Nadima

'Good morning, 7R,' said Mrs C. 'This is Nadima. She hasn't been in the UK very long, and she doesn't speak much English. But I know I can trust you all to look after her and make her feel welcome.'

She nodded at Mr Y, and left, shutting the door behind her firmly, as if she was anxious the girl might want to run away. I wouldn't have blamed her if she did because absolutely *everyone* in 7R was staring at her. Scary or what? Honestly, it was like she was from outer space or something. It was only because she was new. But she stood in the doorway and stared back boldly – bravely even. So when I managed to catch her eye I gave her a big fat welcoming grin. And it was amazing. Her whole face lit up as she grinned back. Then, since the seat next to me was empty, I patted it and gestured to her. She came over and slid into the chair, still giving me that huge grin.

'Hi, I'm Jaz,' I said.

Then she said, 'I am Nadima. Hello.' But she spoke in a really strong accent, sort of like this: 'I-yam Nadeema. Hhhell-o.'

And here's the weird thing. Even though I didn't know anything about her, or what she was like, there was something about her that made me instantly like her. I think it was her guts. You could just tell she was someone who could stick up for herself.

It was great to have someone to sit next to – for a change. The seat next to mine had been empty all term in almost every single class. Lily was my best mate in primary school and she used to sit next to me. But last term she started sitting next to Kara. Don't get me wrong, Lily and I are still mates, and I've lots of other friends, like Chloe and Elly. We're all just one big gang really. So it should all be fine. And it would be – except Kara and I literally *hated* each other at first sight. You have no idea how hard it is being friends with someone who is friends with someone who can't stand you.

Anyhow, Mr Y drifted over and handed Nadima the worksheet about picking our own bedtimes. And then he told me to help her.

Me?!??*!*!

Seriously?!

LOL.

I'm probably the last person on Planet Earth to be able to help *anyone* in English!

I did my best and tried to explain, slowly and clearly, what we were meant to be doing. Nadima nodded politely. But I don't think she understood a single word. Funnily enough, she didn't seem too bothered. Perhaps she was used to it. When the bell rang for break she just gave me a light shrug (and a big grin) and we gathered up our things.

'You can finish off your Persuasive Writing for homework,' Mr Y bellowed as everyone trooped out.

Cue massive groan from everyone (except Nadima of course).

4

Do You Speak Chocolate?

Outside, on the steps by the canteen, everyone clustered round Nadima like hazelnut chips on a Ferrero Rocher. Partly to make her welcome, but mostly because they didn't want to miss anything.

Kara was straight in there.

'Hi! I'm Kara,' she said, flicking her hair around and grabbing centre stage. 'Where are you from?'

Nadima smiled and shrugged apologetically.

'I don't think she understands you,' I said.

Kara shot me a withering look. 'You don't say,' she said. Then she repeated the question more slowly and, get this, *louder*!

'I don't think she's deaf,' I said drily.

Kara ignored me and charged on. 'Do . . . you . . . speak . . . English?'

But before Nadima could even answer Chloe said, 'How long have you been in England?'

And Elly asked, 'Where did you come from?'

And Lily said, 'Where do you live now?'

They *showered* her with questions. It was ridiculous! Nadima just did a lot of smiling and nodding. But she was starting to look a bit dazed.

'Seriously!' I cried. 'Give her a break. It's obvious she can't understand a word you're saying.'

'Well, that's just racist! Assuming she can't speak English!' declared Kara.

'No, it's not!' I said hotly.

'Jaz wasn't being racist,' said Lily calmly.

'Mrs C told us Nadima doesn't speak much English!' I said.

Nadima looked at me when I mentioned her name. I suddenly felt embarrassed, like we were all talking about her as if she wasn't there.

But then Ryan and Liam started leaping around like lunatics, jumping on top of each other until they both fell onto the grass. Where they rolled around wrestling. Clearly to make sure Nadima had noticed them. She grinned at us and rolled her eyes.

'Oh, how very mature,' I said to the boys. Then I looked at Nadima and said, 'Boys, huh!'

'Yes_Boys_Huh!' she repeated, in exactly the

same tone but in her funny accent. Everyone fell about laughing and Nadima smiled at me. Ryan and Liam lay on the ground, grinning like idiots.

'Wait! I've just had a brilliant idea,' said Kara. She whipped out her phone from her back pocket. 'We can use Google Translate!'

'Good idea,' cried Lily, getting her phone out too.

'Yes!' agreed Chloe and Elly, grabbing theirs. I didn't bother. Honestly, Me + Google Translate? I have enough trouble reading English.

Kara's 'brilliant' idea turned out to be a complete non-starter. (Not gloating, just saying.) The basic flaw in her plan was that we didn't actually know which country Nadima was from. And, when we tried asking her, she didn't understand.

'Let's start at the top of the list and work down,' said Kara. She read out the first one. 'Afrikaans.'

'Is that what they speak in Africa?' asked Chloe.

'Must be.' Elly shrugged. I looked at Lily and silently face-palmed. She swallowed a giggle. I was still feeling bad about what I'd said to her earlier, about the shorts. I wanted to say sorry. But I couldn't – not in front of Kara and everybody.

Meanwhile, Chloe was scrolling down the list of

languages on her phone. 'OMG there's hundreds of them!'

'I've never even *heard* of most of them,' said Elly. 'What's this one? Bangla?' She clicked on it.

তুমি কোথা থেকে এসেছ

'Look at that!' she cried, showing us the screen.

So then they all got sidetracked looking at different languages.

Like:

من أي بلد حضرتك

which is Arabic, and:

你从哪里来的

which is Chinese, and:

あなたの出身はどこですか

– Japanese.

All very fascinating – but pointless. Nadima didn't even get a look in. She just stood there looking baffled. I gave her a grin and a big comedy shrug. She grinned and did a big shrug back.

As soon as Kara realised it was going to be impossible to actually *talk* to Nadima she got bored and went off – dragging Lily with her of course. So everyone else drifted after them too.

Soon I was the only one left with Nadima.

There was a horrible long silence while we both looked sheepishly at each other.

'Um . . . *Parlez-vous français?*' I said. Nadima just looked at me.

'Er . . . *Deutsch?*' I tried.

She frowned. I took that as a no. Just as well really, since I don't speak French or German anyway.

There was another, even more awkward silence. Then, in a moment of *brilliant* inspiration, if I say so myself, I dug into my bag and took out a bar of chocolate, broke off a bit and offered it to Nadima.

'Do you speak chocolate?' I said.

Her face did that thing again, when it completely lit up, and her eyes seemed to come to life. She took the chocolate, but before putting it in her mouth she rootled around in her school bag and handed me something wrapped in tin foil. I peeled the foil back and saw a chunk of what looked like Turkish Delight. A very *large* chunk, smothered in icing sugar. I've never been that keen on Turkish Delight to be honest. It's too gooey and chewy. But I ate it to be nice. And OMG it was amazing! It wasn't like the stuff you buy in the shops at all. It was much softer and didn't stick to your teeth and it literally *melted* in your mouth. It was awesome!

We stood there, munching each other's sweets, and at that moment I just knew that even though neither of us could speak a word of each other's language, we were going to be friends. Don't ask me to explain how. I can't. But I just knew.

5
Text Me?

I didn't get a chance to say sorry to Lily all day.
So as soon as I got in after school I texted her.

Im sory I was hrid to yuo. Txt me bk?

Which autocorrect miraculously turned into:

I'm sorry I was horrid to you. Text me back?

I waited a few moments, but she didn't reply. Lil's
not one of those people who goes off on a sulk.
(Not like some others I could mention. No points
for guessing who.) If she wasn't talking to me then
I must have really upset her. So I decided that if
she didn't text back I'd give her a call later.

Thursday is my night to cook supper. I put a
pack of pasta on to boil, opened three tins of tuna

and grated a small mountain of cheese. Honestly, The Brothers eat a *ridonkulous* amount of food. It's all the sports they do. I threw together a tuna pasta bake and shoved it in the oven. Then I checked my phone again. Still no reply from Lily.

Thursdays are also, btw, the best night of the *entire* week. Gus has football training, Dan does rugby and Matt goes to karate (like he does pretty much every night). The Brothers are all *unbelievably* sporty and the hall mirror is *covered* with their medals. I literally haven't won a medal since Lily and I won the three-legged race when I was about six. But Mum keeps the lot. One of these days that mirror's going to fall off the wall – pulled down under the weight of our family's amazing achievements.

LOL.

So straight after school on Thursdays, The Brothers all zoom in, grab their kits and rush straight back out again. Then they're out for about two hours – until Mum picks them up on her way back from work.

Which leaves me all alone – *with the computer*! Matt's the only one who's got his own laptop – so I'm always having to fight Gus and Dan to get a go on the one in the kitchen. Mum's *promised* me one – in Year 12! That's five years away! I can't wait that long because, fyi, I've got a business to launch. I sat down at the computer and opened up the website I was designing.

It might interest you to know that absolutely *loads* of incredibly successful entrepreneurs are dyslexic. Lord Alan Sugar (off *The Apprentice*) is, and so's the woman who set up The Body Shop. Then there's Richard Branson and Jamie Oliver . . . and the bloke who started Ikea. (I don't know his name – and I probably couldn't spell it if I did.) I'm determined to be one of them.

I've run loads of business schemes. Last summer I sold home-made cupcakes and lemonade outside our house, which was pretty successful. Then I tried hiring The Brothers out for babysitting and washing cars, which was *not* successful. Partly because the boys weren't keen on handing over my fee (ten per cent of their earnings), but mostly because they weren't that keen on working *at all*.

Anyhow, I have lots of ideas, but my best one at the moment is setting up a website for kids to flog off all their old games and clothes. Then they can use the money they make to buy new stuff and so, *and here's the clever bit*, all the gaming shops and clothes stores will want to advertise on the site – which is how I'll make the money. Genius or what?

But I can't run a business without my own computer.

I'm working on it.

I checked my phone again. Still no reply from Lily. I bet Kara had told her to ignore me. So I tried calling – but Lil didn't pick up. Just then I heard Mum's key in the lock and suddenly The Brothers charged into the kitchen like a herd of starving elephants.

'Mmmm, smells good,' said Mum, following them in and giving me a hug.

'Give me FOOOOD!' yelled Gus, shoving past me and hurling himself in his chair.

'What's for supper?' demanded Matt, climbing over Gus to get to his place.

'Tuna pasta bake,' I announced.

'Please tell me you didn't put peas in it,' begged Dan, ducking under the table to get to his seat.

'I put peas in it,' I said cheerfully, putting the dish on the table.

'Noooooo!' groaned Dan, emerging on the other side.

'Oh, man up and eat your greens.' I grinned.

Mum sat calmly in her place, ignoring the chaos all around her.

'Looks lovely, darling. Thank you,' she said, picking up the serving spoon and ladling out the pasta.

Btw, it was *delicious* – if I say so myself.

'So, good day at school, everyone?' asked Mum as we all tucked in.

'Perfect,' replied Matt, shooting me a dark look. 'The skirts were an absolute triumph,' he said flatly.

'Ah,' said Mum.

'Yeah, I particularly enjoyed getting rinsed by Mrs C,' said Dan.

'Not to mention getting to spend the *entire* day in someone else's disgusting old clothes,' groaned Gus.

'Yeah, thanks, sis,' said Dan.

'It's not my fault!' I protested. 'How was I to know Mrs C was going to make us raid the lost property.'

'I'm sure something bit me.' Gus shuddered, frantically scratching his legs.

Mum grimaced. 'So, rubbish day all round then?'

'Not completely,' I said, and I told her about Nadima.

'Where's she from?' asked Matt.

'Dunno. She doesn't speak enough English to ask her.'

'That must be hard,' said Mum, 'spending all day with people you can't understand.'

'Just like being with the girls in my class,' said Dan.

'Probably a bit scary too,' Mum went on.

'Again, just like being with the girls in my class,' said Dan. Matt grinned at him.

'I hope everyone's being friendly to her,' said Mum. 'Trying to make her welcome, helping her fit in.'

I thought about Kara trying to use Google Translate. But then I remembered how everyone had drifted off when they realised they couldn't actually talk to Nadima. Which was a bit mean, come to think of it.

'She's dead keen to learn English,' I said. 'She kept pointing at things like the stairs or a bench and saying, "What is please?" So I spent the whole day telling her the names of stuff. I felt like a walking talking dictionary!'

'Just don't tell her how to spell anything,' said Gus.

'Oh, ha very ha,' I said.

'Gus – that's not funny,' said Mum with a warning look.

Gus tried giving me a grin, but I ignored him. I don't mind them teasing me about my spelling and stuff, but sometimes I'm just not in the mood. I was fed up that my shorts protest had been such an epic fail, plus I really wanted Lily to text me back.

If she wasn't talking to me, then tomorrow was going to be a really rubbish day.

6
Melodrama!

We were about halfway to school when Mum suddenly realised she'd left her house brochures on the kitchen table.

'Damn, damn, damn!' she cried, slamming on the brakes. All around us, tyres screeched and horns blared.

'Death by school run' is definitely the downside of having an estate agent for a mum. She's always trying to get us to school *and* get to her first appointment *at exactly the same time*.

'All right, all right!' She promptly started doing a three-point-turn – in the middle of the rush-hour traffic!

'Muuuum!' I wailed, clinging onto my seat.

'Sorry, but I've got an appointment right after I drop you off. You're all just going to have to be a bit late.'

'For a change,' muttered Dan.

The school looked deserted by the time we finally got there. So I clutched my bag to my chest and *ran*. I was cutting through the English block, racing down the corridor, when a voice bellowed, 'Jaz Watson! No running!'

Guess who it was? My arch-enemy, Mr Y.

'But I'm late, sir!' I cried.

'Whose fault is that?'

'Well, actually, not mine, sir! My mum . . .'

He held up his hand. 'Spare me the excuses – believe me, I've heard them all.'

'But, sir, if I don't run, then I'll be late for registration.'

'Very probably, but right now you're in trouble for running in the corridor. And if you stand there answering me back you'll probably be late for registration too,' he finished smugly. 'Now run along. And WALK!'

Honestly?! *Run along and walk?* How is that even humanly possible?!

Fortunately Mrs W wasn't even in the room by the time I rushed in. Just as well – everyone was chatting and laughing and mucking about and the noise level was *off the scale*. Ryan and Liam were throwing pens at one another, while Liam spun round and round in Mrs W's whirly chair. Nadima was already sitting in the seat next to mine. She smiled when she saw me, but she looked a bit shocked at the chaos raging all around her.

Lily and Kara were sitting on their table, with Elly and Chloe as usual. They were all singing along to something on Kara's phone. Lily shoved over to make room for me on the corner of the table so I squatted on the edge. Nadima's face fell. I felt bad – but I needed to talk to Lily.

'I tried texting you, and calling, but you didn't pick up,' I said, but *quietly*, hoping big-ears Kara wouldn't hear.

'Sorry, my phone died,' said Lily, pulling a face.

'Oh, was that all?'

She shot me a questioning look.

'I thought you were mad at me for being horrible to you about the shorts thing,' I said.

'What?! No! Of course I wasn't, you spanner!' She grinned.

I grinned back at her sheepishly. 'I'm sorry,' I said. She smiled and shrugged.

I was so relieved. Maybe it wasn't going to be such a rubbish day after all.

But just at that moment Chloe said something about the Persuasive Writing homework and I gasped out loud. I'd completely forgotten to do it.

'OMG Mr Y's going to slaughter me! When's English?'

'Don't panic.' Lily laughed. 'You can do it at lunchtime. I'll give you a hand.'

Out of the corner of my eye I saw Kara rolling her eyes – I ignored her.

'Thanks, Lil!' Then I added, 'I'm going to sit next to Nadima. OK? She's all on her own.'

'Sure,' said Lily. I slid into my own seat – and Nadima's face lit up.

The mention of the English homework had launched Kara into one of her mega-melodramas.

'It was *terrible*,' she announced to the *entire* class (obviously assuming *everyone* would be *fascinated*.) 'I had this *massive* row with my stepdad about it. He *literally* told me he's got the right to tell me when to go to bed!'

'What?! He's not even your dad!' cried Chloe.

'It's not up to him,' added Lily.

'Who does he think he is?' said Elly, not wanting to miss her turn at whipping up the drama.

'I know! I gave him a right mouthful, and then

Mum had a go at *me*,' said Kara. Then she put her head on Lily's shoulder 'sadly' and added, 'I hate my life.' Lily put her arm round her.

'OMG! You're so over the top, Kara!' I laughed. 'It's not like he dragged you to your room at half past six, threw you in and locked the door!'

Kara shot me a filthy look. 'You don't know anything about my life!' she snapped.

Honestly, you'd think she was the only one ever to have a stepdad, the way she goes on about it. It's like she's Snow White or something.

7
Fa-toosh

Nadima stuck to me like glue as we traipsed from class to class, which, btw, given the size of our school, was very wise. I seriously thought about drawing her a map.

All the other kids were chattering away, but Nadima and I just walked along silently, exchanging the odd smile – but it wasn't awkward or anything. When we got to each class I told her which lesson it was and showed her which books to get out. Which, frankly, was about all the help I could give her.

It was a typical Friday morning (yawn): double science (double yawn) followed by history (huge YAWN) and then French (*zzzzz*). I had no idea if Nadima actually understood any of the lessons. (But then that wouldn't make her any different from most of 7R.) But she soon gave up trying to make any notes.

French must have been a complete nightmare for her. I mean, how on earth is she supposed to cope with learning French *in English* when she can't understand English? It would be like me trying to learn Italian *in Russian* or something. *Ridonkulous!* Plus our French teacher is rubbish. She just reads stuff out from the board. She's about as much use as a chocolate teaspoon. And it's so *boring*. After about five minutes I'd completely zoned out and was thinking up names for my web business. Something catchy, you know, like 'Amazon' or 'Gumtree'. Then I started wondering why 'Amazon' was called 'Amazon', and why 'Gumtree' was called 'Gumtree'. What even is a gumtree?

But the bell *finally* went for the end of the lesson and we headed off to lunch. Lily and Kara and everyone were sitting together in the canteen, but I just wasn't in the mood for Kara, especially after she'd had a go at me earlier on. So I took Nadima off to sit under the trees along the side of the back field.

Loads of kids were outside on the grass eating, or messing around. We leaned with our backs against a tree trunk in the cool, and got out our lunch boxes. I offered mine to Nadima to have a taste.

'What is?' she asked.

'Tuna pasta mayo.'

'Tuna . . . pasta . . . mayo,' she repeated before putting the fork in her mouth. She chewed for a moment and then said, 'Mmmm! Is good. I like!'

'Thank you! Made by my own fair hands,' I told her.

She frowned so I said slowly, 'I made it.'

'Ah!' She nodded, understanding. Then she offered me a taste of hers.

'Mum make,' she said.

It was some sort of salad thing, with chunks of tomatoes, peppers and cucumber – and torn up bits of pitta bread. I took a forkful. The salad bits were crunchy but the bread was soft and literally *dripping* with dressing. An explosion of lemon and spices hit my tongue.

'OMG it's fabulous!' I mumbled, with my mouth full.

Nadima's eyes shone. 'Is fattoush.' She grinned.

'Fa-toosh.' I repeated. 'Your mum is a brilliant cook,' I said, helping myself to another forkful.

After we'd eaten I got out my phone. 'Swap numbers?' I said. She shrugged, not understanding me, so I mimed texting and pointed at each of us.

33

'Ah! Yes!' She nodded.

Then we spent the rest of lunch looking at *ridonkulously* cute pictures of cats and dogs until the bell went for afternoon registration. It was really good fun. It still felt a bit odd, not being able to have a proper conversation, but we had a good laugh, and we seemed to like the same things. Except I think I'm more of a dog person and she's more into cats. But who cares?!

Straight after lunch it was English. The *second* I sat down I remembered I hadn't done the stupid Persuasive Writing homework at lunchtime. I groaned out loud, but there was nothing I could do about it. Mr Y was going to kill me.

'That's the third time this term,' he glared at me. And I'm pretty sure he smirked when he added, 'I'm afraid that means a letter home.'

I gasped. Mum was going to go ape. 'Can't I just do it tonight?' I begged.

'Nope. You should have done it last night.'

'But that's just really harsh!' I wailed.

'That's enough!'

'But, sir –'

'One more word out of you and I'll put you on report,' he warned.

I shut up. The rest of the class went deathly quiet. Then Mr Y glanced at Nadima and then back at me. 'I hope you're not going to be a bad influence on our new arrival.'

How unfair was that?! I was speechless. Which was probably just as well. Because if I went on report Mum would *literally* murder me.

8
Invitations

On Saturdays I'm usually the first downstairs. Mainly so that I can grab the computer before The Brothers, but partly so I can get first pick of whatever Mum's got in for weekend breakfasts before it all disappears into one brother or another. This morning it was waffles! Fyi, I like them hot, toasted and plastered with chocolate spread. But who doesn't?! So I sat there in my PJs, happily licking chocolate spread off my fingers and trying to solve a problem on my website.

It's easy enough to set up a website. Any dorkbrain can do it. But I was trying to figure out how to set one up where *other* people could upload stuff and not just me – like on eBay or Gumtree. I didn't want everything going through me. I'd spend all my time posting ads for people.

Just at that moment two things happened:

a) I heard the letter box flap in the front door and

b) I remembered the homework letter.

For a nano-second I seriously thought about rushing along the hall and grabbing it before anyone saw it. (By which I mean Mum.) But then I heard her padding down the stairs. She paused by the front door. Not a good sign. She usually scoops up the post and brings it into the kitchen – unless there's something interesting . . . or unusual . . . in which case she opens it there and then by the front door.

I held my breath.

'JAZ!' she bellowed, striding furiously into the kitchen.

'I can explain!' I cried.

She stopped to flick the kettle on and then she turned and waved the letter at me angrily. 'You forgot your English homework *again*.'

'I didn't mean to. I was going to do it at lunchtime – with Lily. But she was busy.'

'Too busy to help you? That doesn't sound like Lily. Did you even ask her?' she challenged.

'Yes, I did!' I protested.

And yes, I *know* I was sort of fudging the truth. But I didn't want to admit that I'd forgotten to do it lunchtime. And besides, the *reason* I forgot was because Lily was with Kara, and Kara had been horrible to me – so it wasn't actually my fault, was it?

Mum sighed. Then she made two mugs of tea and handed me one.

'Save what you're doing, and leave the computer for a minute,' she said, sitting down opposite me at the table. My heart sank.

'None of the boys has *ever* had a letter home about not doing homework, Jaz,' she said. 'And it's your English. Again.' Then she said, 'Sweetheart, is this because of your dyslexia?'

'No! It's not! It's because Mr Y doesn't like me! He's always picking on me. You can ask Lily. Ask anyone!'

Mum took a slurp of tea and thought for a moment. 'My maths teacher hated me,' she said, 'and I hated him back!' She took another swig of tea before adding, 'So I made sure I did my maths homework so he *couldn't* have a go at me.'

'I meant to do it – I honestly just forgot,' I said. Which was true.

'Do you want me to talk to him?'

I shook my head. 'It'll only make it worse.'

'You're probably right. So what are you going to do to make sure you *don't* forget your homework again?'

Fyi, dyslexics are *brilliant* at coming up with strategies. Seriously. It's probably because we have to get round about a zillion problems every day. I don't get sidetracked, or bogged down in all the little details like other people do. I'm better at solving the big problems. And I look at things differently. I'm nearly always the one who comes up with new and *original* ideas. Some of the *greatest geniuses* of all time were dyslexic – Albert Einstein, Leonardo da Vinci, Steve Jobs, even Walt Disney.

So I thought for a moment then said, 'One, I'll put my English book on my bed to remind me to do it today. Two, I'll see which days I have English. And then three, I'll set up a reminder on my phone, on those days, to check I've done my homework.'

'Sounds like a fine upstanding plan,' said Mum, getting up from the table. 'Fancy a cooked breakfast?' she added, opening the fridge. 'Eggs? Bacon? Hash browns? Mushrooms?'

'Bring it on!' I said, ignoring the fact I'd already

demolished two waffles and a bucket of chocolate spread, and we started cooking it together. Pretty soon the smell of bacon drifted upstairs, so The Brothers drifted downstairs.

9
Plans

'I'm starving!' announced Matt, clattering into his chair.

'Don't just sit down – grab the knives and forks!' said Mum, buttering a mound of toast.

'Dan, knives and forks!' said Matt, not moving.

'I'm busy!' said Dan, trying to nick a slice of bacon out of the frying pan as he passed me at the cooker.

'Oi!' I smacked his hand away with the wooden spatula.

Gus sat himself down in front of the computer.

'I'm on that!' I told him.

'No, you're not. You're frying bacon,' he said.

'I'm logged in!'

'No, you're not!' he said, promptly logging me off.

'Well, I'm having it after breakfast.'

'Again, no, you're not.'

'Muuum!' I wailed.

'Gus . . .' appealed Mum.

'She's already had a turn!' he exclaimed. 'It's my go.'

'And I'm after Gus!' claimed Dan.

See? Seriously! What chance have I got to get my business started?

'Why can't I have my *own* computer!' I cried.

'Because I'm not a millionaire!' replied Mum.

'Ah! But if you get me a laptop, then I can set up my website and *I'll* be a millionaire,' I said, with dazzling logic. 'I'll pay you back!' I promised.

Mum just rolled her eyes.

'Nice try, Jaz!' said Matt.

'Tuck in!' announced Mum, plonking the frying pans onto the table. Everyone started helping themselves. Gus and Dan *literally* had a fork fight for the last hash brown.

Mum ignored them. 'Is Lily coming over today?' she asked me.

'No, she's busy.'

'What's she up to?'

'Shopping – with Kara.'

Mum shot me a look. I ignored it. 'What about Chloe and Elly?' she asked brightly.

'I think they're busy too,' I said.

'Oh. Well, in that case you can muck out your room!'

'Golly, thanks, Mum. What a treat!' I said, as sarcastically as I could.

After a while she said, 'Tell you what, why don't you invite everyone over next weekend? Have a camp-out.'

'Maybe just Lily,' I said.

'Have everyone!' urged Mum. 'It'll be more fun.'

Hang on, I thought. I could see what Mum was up to. So I said, 'I'm not inviting Kara.'

'Jaz, this is not the way to handle this,' she said. 'You have to invite Kara.'

'But she's horrible to me,' I told her. 'You always tell us to stick up for ourselves and not let people push us around. How is it "sticking up for myself" if she takes Lily off me and I just let her get away with it?'

'You can't punish Kara just because Lily wants to be friends with her instead of you,' said Matt.

'The best thing you can do is try to make friends with Kara too,' said Mum.

'That's impossible! We don't even like each

other!' I cried. 'If I have to have Kara, then I'm not having a camp-out,' I announced. And I really meant it.

'Fine,' said Mum. And she really meant it too. There was a bit of a pause and then Mum said, 'How's your new friend Nadima getting on?'

'Fine, I think,' I replied, still feeling grumpy.

'Why don't you ask her round after school one evening?' she said.

'How am I supposed to do that? She doesn't actually speak English,' I pointed out.

'Not any?'

'Well, only a bit.'

'Then keep it simple. Maybe she can understand more than you think she can.'

'Or maybe she can understand less than *you* think she can,' I replied.

'Oh, come on, you! You're good at getting round problems,' said Mum.

'I don't really know her *that* well. It might look a bit weird,' I said. 'A bit pushy.'

'Or it might look a bit friendly,' she responded. 'A bit, you know, "nice", or "kind", or "welcoming".'

I could see she wasn't going to give up so I said, 'Fine.'

'Any day except Monday,' announced Dan. That's because he cooks on Mondays. (Burgers.)

'Or Tuesday,' said Gus which is, yup, you've guessed it, his night to cook. (Bangers and mash.)

'Or Wednesday,' added Matt. (Spag bol.)

'You'd better not have her over on a Thursday,' said Dan. 'Not if you want her to like you. Food poisoning can be very off-putting.'

'Ha, very, ha ha!' I said.

'Invite her on a Friday,' said Mum. 'This Friday, if you like.'

'OK,' I said, although frankly I still wasn't sure if it was a good idea.

10
Emojis

After breakfast I sloped upstairs to do my English homework. But before I threw myself into that absolutely *thrilling* task, I tried to work out how to invite Nadima for supper on Friday.

It was a bit of a challenge but then, being dyslexic, I like a challenge. They bring out the best in me. Fyi, loads of awesome celebrities are dyslexic. Keanu Reeves, Kiera Knightley, Orlando Bloom, Whoopi Goldberg, Tom Cruise, Winston Churchill . . . (Not that he's a celebrity. But I suppose he was, so he still counts.)

I could go on. Honestly, being dyslexic is like being in an exclusive club.

Anyhow, back to the problem of how to invite Nadima to supper.

I picked up my phone, and, after a lot of typing and deleting and thinking about which English words she might actually know, and which words I can actually spell, I sent her this:

 Friday **?** 👍 👎
Jaz

Then I added a link to my address on Google Maps and hit send. Clever or what? Frankly, I thought it was the work of a genius.

A few minutes later she replied.

Nad

And it suddenly hit me: *Everyone can read emojis!*

So I sent her this:

🎶 **?**

She replied:

So I sent this:

And she sent back:

Do I like reading?! I thought *Noooooo!*

Jaz x

Nad

I laughed and replied:

J

N

J

N

I grinned and sent:

followed by:

LOL!

It was brilliant. I don't know why we didn't think of using emojis before!

11

❧Kurdî❧

When I swung into our form room on Monday morning I was looking forward to seeing Nadima. I was expecting to find her sitting calmly in her seat next to mine. She wasn't. She was busy hauling Liam out of the waste bin. For some strange reason, best known to himself, Liam had tried to sit in it – and now he couldn't get out. Obviously everyone else in the class was too busy laughing at him to be any help – especially Ryan. So Nadima was the only one to come to his rescue.

'Liam! You complete wally!' I laughed, as she pulled on his hands, and I hung onto the bin.

'Thanks, Nadima,' he gushed.

'Oi!' I said.

'Oh, you too, Jaz,' he added.

Boys, Huh! I thought.

Just then, Chloe came rushing into the room and immediately started handing out invitations.

'I'm having a movie party for my birthday,' she squealed.

'Oooh!' cried Kara, ripping open her envelope. Lily and the others tore theirs open too. Pink sparkly glitter scattered *everywhere*.

'Oops!' giggled Chloe. 'I forgot to warn you!'

Honestly, that girl should come with a permanent glitter warning.

'You muppet!' laughed Lily, brushing a shower of the stuff off her polo shirt.

I deliberately didn't open mine because Nadima hadn't got one and I didn't want to make her feel left out. I could see she was trying to put a brave face on it.

Kara read hers and suddenly wailed, 'Oh NO! I can't go!'

'Why not?' Chloe's face fell.

'I'll be at my dad's!'

'Can't he bring you?' asked Lily. Which seemed a fair question, since Kara's dad only lives a few miles away.

'I can't possibly ask him! I only get to see him every other weekend,' cried Kara. Then turning to

51

Chloe she said (with *spectacular* selfishness), 'Can't you make it the next weekend?'

'Um . . . I'm not sure,' said Chloe. 'Mum works weekends and she had to book the time off.'

'Oh, pleeese!' begged Kara. 'Pleeeeese!' and she did this silly pleading gesture. 'I don't want to be the only one who can't come! Please!'

Chloe looked gutted. Honestly, Kara expects the entire world to fit around her. She's *always* going on about how dreadful her life is because her parents are divorced, and how she only gets to see her dad every other weekend, and how much she misses him. I don't even have a dad. Mine went off just after I was born so I don't actually remember him at all. But I don't go round making a big thing of it.

So I said, 'Seriously, Kara?! You can't expect Chloe's mum to change her weekend off. Surely your dad won't mind you going to the movies for a couple of hours. It's not like you won't see him at all that weekend. What's the problem?'

She whirled round at me. 'I can't believe you just said that to me! You can't even begin to imagine how much I miss my dad – and if you did you wouldn't be so horrible.' And she made her eyes well up like she was going to cry. Honestly, she's such a drama queen.

So naturally, Lil felt she had to put her arm round her.

And poor Chloe felt she had to say, 'Of course I'll ask Mum if we can change the date. I want everyone to be able to come.'

'Thank you!' said Kara, giving her a hug.

'Chloe? Talking about missing people out . . .' I said quietly, 'I wondered if Nadima could come too?'

'It's a movie party!' said Elly. 'She won't understand the film.'

'So? I just think it would be nice to include her.'

'You can't go round inviting people to someone else's party,' said Kara. 'It's rude.'

'I'm not,' I said coolly. 'I'm asking Chloe to invite her.'

Chloe looked at Kara, like she wasn't sure what to do.

But then Lil said, 'Go on, Chloe. Nadima can probably follow the story from the action.

As usual, at the mention of her name, Nadima looked up and everyone felt very uncomfortable, even me.

So Chloe said, 'Sure! I'll make another invitation and bring it in tomorrow.'

'Why don't you just put "and Nadima" on mine?' I suggested.

'Doh, why I didn't think of that?!' Chloe laughed.

(Probably because you're not dyslexic, so you're not as good at solving problems as I am, I thought. But I didn't say that, *obviously*.)

She took my envelope back from me, tore it open (Cue pink glitter flying *everywhere*), wrote '+ Nadima', with a little heart over the 'i', and handed it to Nadima.

Nadima looked at the invitation and then at me. Obviously she could read her own name, and mine too. She'd have had to be an idiot not to realise she'd been invited to something – but she didn't know what.

She got out her phone and typed into it quickly, and then her whole face lit up and she said, 'Ah! Is birthday. Yes?'

'Yes!' we all cried.

'Wait! Wait! Give me your phone!' I grabbed it. She was using Google Translate so I'd be able to see which language she spoke!

The only flaw in the plan was that I couldn't

actually read the name of her language. Mostly because it was a completely new word to me. I can usually make a good guess at a word if it's one I know, but I'd never seen this word before.

It said:

> Kurdî?

I stood looking at it blankly.

Then Kara snatched the phone out of my hand.

'Hey! I was looking at that!'

She ignored me. 'Kurdî?' she read.

'Kurdy? I've never even heard of it!' said Chloe.

'Me neither,' said Elly. 'Where do they speak Kurdy?'

'I've heard of Kurd*ish* but not Kurdy,' said Lily. 'Hang on! Maybe "Kurdy" is Kurdish for "Kurdish"!'

'What, like "English" is English for "English"?' said Chloe.

We all snorted with laughter – including Chloe when she realised what she'd said.

'Honestly, Chloe!' Lily giggled.

Then Kara turned to Nadima and, I'm not joking, actually said, 'Is "Kurdy" Kurdish for "Kurdish"?'

'How's she supposed to understand that?' I cried.

'I'm only trying to help!' Kara snapped.

'How is that helping?! Asking her rubbish questions like that?'

She turned on me furiously. 'It's not a rubbish question! You just don't want other people making friends with her.'

'That's not true!' I gasped, but Kara flounced off, and the others followed her. I stood there speechless with fury. *Kara's* the one who doesn't like people being friends with anyone else except her. *Especially* Lily.

12
Drama

First thing after registration it was drama (snore, snore) so we all trudged off to the English block. I hung back with Nadima, because I was so angry with Kara. I don't know if Nadima had actually understood what Kara had said, but she obviously knew she'd had a go at me because she smiled and shrugged sympathetically. I tried to smile back.

As soon as we walked into the studio Mrs P, our drama teacher, literally *pounced* on Nadima. She isn't a particularly large woman, but she wears these enormous multicoloured kaftans. She looks like a circus tent on legs – and she never stops talking.

'You're new!' she trilled.

'She doesn't miss much, does she?' whispered Lily. I grinned. It would be hard to miss Nadima, since she's the only one in our form wearing a hijab.

Mrs P ploughed on. 'Hello, hello! And how absolutely *lovely* to have someone new,' she gushed.

Nadima shot me a startled look, but there was no escaping Mrs P in full flow.

'I know it's probably a bit difficult moving schools in the middle of the year, but actually it's *perfect timing* because we're starting a really exciting new project today and everyone has to be in pairs,' Mrs P went on.

Out of the corner of my eye, I saw Kara nod at Lily to indicate they were a pair. I ignored them.

'But we had an odd number of pupils in the class, and so someone was either going to be left out, or we'd have to have a group of three,' carried on Mrs P to Nadima, 'but now that you've joined us everyone can pair up, can't they? So that makes it nice and neat. Excellent! So, welcome, welcome and . . . sorry, what did you say your name was?'

Nadima didn't answer. Her eyes slid to me and then back to Mrs P. The entire class was desperately trying not to laugh.

'Hmmm?' prompted Mrs P, staring questioningly at Nadima.

I stepped forward to rescue both of them. 'This

is Nadima. She doesn't speak much English,' I said flatly.

Poor Mrs P. Her entire welcoming speech had been a complete waste of time. We knew it, she knew it and – worse – she knew we knew it. Her face fell – and the whole class exploded in laughter.

Anyhow, fyi, the 'really exciting new project' turned out to be a really boring storytelling thing, which we were going to spend *the whole of the rest of the term on*. We had to make up a story about 'A Box' for some reason. A box. Why? Honestly, where do they get their ideas from? And *then* we were going to have to perform it for the whole class at the end of term.

Oh, how absolutely brilliant.

I don't like stories. I don't like acting and I'd rather eat deep-fried maggots *every day* for the rest of term than stand up in front of 7R and act out some rubbish story.

Again, how absolutely brilliant.

By now the rest of the class was busily sorting themselves into pairs. Kara had nabbed Lily, and Chloe and Elly had paired up. So I grabbed Nadima's arm and took her off to find a space. We sat cross-legged on the grubby floor. We were meant to come up with the basic idea for our stories, so everyone around us was chattering away and writing stuff down.

I looked at Nadima and she looked back at me.

She had ABSOLUTELY NO IDEA what we were meant to be doing, and I had ABSOLUTELY NO IDEA how to explain.

Oh, how ABSOLUTELY BRILLIANT. Not.

Mrs P was going around checking that everyone was actually working on their stories – rather than gossiping, texting and watching YouTube. (Yup, she's got a pretty good handle on 7R.)

'How're you getting on?' she asked, bounding over to Nadima and me, like a puppy in fancy dress.

'Are you coming up with lots of brilliant story ideas?' she went on hopefully.

Nadima looked at her blankly. Politely, but blankly.

I took a deep breath and said, 'It's a bit hard to do that since, as I said earlier, Nadima doesn't actually speak much English.'

'Well, perhaps you can *mime* something,' Mrs P said brightly. 'Use your imaginations!' she trilled, and then whirled away in a swirl of colour, to talk to superstar Kara and her supporting actress, Lily.

Fyi, Kara's been in a drama club pretty much since she was born – as far as I can make out. Possibly even earlier. She's got an agent and everything, and last term she was in a TV ad. Yes – those are her legs you can see, giving an award-winning performance, running up a flight of stairs in the advert for *Spot-It-Off* carpet stain remover. (Next stop, Hollywood. Well, they have Really Big Carpets over there, don't they? Red ones.)

I waited until Mrs P had moved on to another pair, and then shuffled over to Kara and Lily to see what 'the expert' was doing. Nadima followed me, dragging our bags with her.

'We need somewhere *really* dramatic,' Kara was saying, and then she gasped melodramatically and flapped her hands at Lily. 'Oh, I know! How about she finds the baby – *in the snow*?!'

'Oh, that's a really good idea.' Lily nodded.

'Or in a public toilet?' I cut in.

'A toilet. Why would you leave a baby in a toilet?' snapped Kara.

'So that someone would find it,' I replied, with stunning logic, if I say so myself. 'Plus, it's less likely to freeze to death.'

61

'Oh, for goodness sake!' spluttered Kara. 'It's a dramatic storytelling. Not an episode of *EastEnders*!'

I shrugged.

'What's your story about?' asked Lily.

'We haven't actually come up with one yet,' I said.

'You mean, *you* haven't,' said Kara. 'You can't expect Nadima to, can you?'

Nadima looked up at the mention of her name and gave Kara a questioning stare. Quite a *hard* questioning stare actually. And she held it for an uncomfortably long time. Go, Nadima! I thought. I *knew* she was going to be someone who could stand up for herself!

Kara flushed pink. 'I hope you haven't come over to nick our ideas, Jaz,' she said, obviously deciding that attack was the best form of defence.

Huh, I thought, we'd have to be pretty desperate if we couldn't come up with something better than finding a baby in the snow.

'I've got plenty of ideas, thanks. And I bet Nadima has too. Just because she can't speak English doesn't mean she's stupid.'

'She didn't say she was!' said Lily.

'Yeah! You used the s-word – not me,' said Kara smugly.

By now Lily was looking dead embarrassed because Nadima had folded her arms and was giving them *both* a challenging look. At which point the bell went. Lily shot me an apologetic look, but she still followed after Kara as they got their bags and left. Nadima handed me my bag and we trailed after them.

Somehow I'd managed to end up rowing with Lily and Kara again. Oh, how absolutely brilliant. How does that even keep happening?

13
Genius!

After Kara's mega-melodrama about Chloe's birthday party, a *brilliant* idea struck me. If Kara was going to be away at her dad's, then next weekend would be the *perfect* time to invite everyone to a camp-out at my house. *And* Mum wouldn't be able to have a go at me for leaving her out. Then I could get proper time with Lily – without Kara. Genius or what?!

I didn't want to make it too obvious, so I left it for a couple of days and then grabbed everyone after registration, as we all walked along the corridor to class (geography, fyi).

'I'm having a camp-out on Saturday,' I said casually. 'Who's up for it? Lily?'

'Yeah!' she cried. She loves camping.

'Chloe? Elly?' They both grinned and nodded. Then I paused before adding, 'Kara?'

'You know I can't come,' she said. 'I'm going to my dad's. Remember?'

'Oh! Sorry! I completely forgot!' I lied. Kara put on a 'sad' face and Lily flashed me a look. So, because I didn't want Lily to think I was deliberately leaving Kara out (even though I was) I said, 'Oh, well, you can come another time.'

Kara was furious. I was feeling pretty smart until she suddenly said, 'What about Nadima? Aren't you inviting Nadima?'

And everyone looked at Nadima, and Nadima looked at me.

I suddenly felt awful. I hadn't planned to invite Nadima, as she was coming round to mine on Friday anyway. I honestly thought she'd find it really hard spending a *whole* night in a tent with a bunch of people she could hardly talk to. But I could see now how it looked, to the others.

'Well, I think it's pretty mean of you to invite everyone else in front of her and leave her out,' said Kara. 'Especially when you made such a fuss about Chloe inviting her to *her* party!'

'I'm not leaving Nadima out!' I cried. 'She's coming round after school on Friday.' And then I saw the look on Lily's face. She looked really surprised, and then hurt. Which was stupid. She must have had Kara round loads of times without me. But even so, somehow I'd managed to upset Lily *and* I'd given Kara something to gloat about. Oh, brilliant. Just brilliant.

On the way home on the bus I texted Lily:

I'm sorry I didn't tell you Nadima was coming round

> Why? It's not up to me!

Are you mad at me

> No

I was pretty sure she was lying. Especially when she added:

Did you deliberately invite us for a camp-out when Kara couldn't come?

> No

I lied. I don't think she believed me. I texted:

Are you still coming

> Yes

Which should have made me feel better.

It didn't.

I thought about texting Nad – but I couldn't work out what to put. I could hardly ask her if she was upset that I hadn't invited her to a camp-out which I didn't know if she knew I was even having, could I? Even if you could say all that with emojis – which you obviously can't.

Why was just being friends with everyone getting so complicated?

14

Pizza

Friday after school, Nadima came home with me on the school bus. All around us the other kids were chatting or laughing and mucking about. Someone was chucking someone else's pencil case around. Nadima and I ducked as it flew over our heads. We sat there in silence for a while and it started to feel a bit awkward. I had no idea if Nadima knew about the camp-out on Saturday. She hadn't said anything about it if she did. So I decided to just leave it.

So I got out my phone and we looked at animals doing daft things like skateboarding and surfing or driving cars. Some of them *must* have been Photoshopped, especially the waterskiing hippopotamus, but who cares? They were *hilarious*! We were crying with laughter by the time the bus stopped.

*

When we got to the front door, Mum came bustling down the hall to meet us. She must've got off work especially early.

Nadima stood in the doorway. She suddenly seemed a bit shy. I'd never seen her like that before.

'Mind your backs, girls, coming through,' said Matt, as The Brothers pushed between us on their way in and slogged upstairs to dump their bags in their rooms, their long legs taking the stairs two at a time.

Mum gave Nad a huge welcoming grin. 'Hello! You must be Nadima. I'm Kate, Jaz's mum. Come in, come in,' she said.

But Nadima just stood there on the doorstep. Then she took a deep breath and said, 'Hello. I am Nadima. I am very happy to meet you. Thank you for inviting me to your lovely home. It is very kind of you.'

It was really funny – like a formal speech. It all came tumbling out as if she'd been practising it for days. Which, come to think of it, she probably had. I'd literally never heard Nadima say so much English in one go before. It was pretty impressive!

Mum didn't bat an eyelid. She just said, 'You're most welcome,' and then she took Nadima's school bag off her and I dragged Nad upstairs.

As soon as we got into my room we collapsed into giggles.

Then Nadima insisted on playing 'What is please?' with the *entire contents* of my room. So I stood there, like a talking dictionary, for about half an hour going 'Bed . . . pillow . . . quilt . . . wardrobe . . . desk . . . chair . . . poster . . . books . . . clothes . . . trainers . . . curtains . . . while she pointed and studiously repeated every word. Honestly, she's like a sponge when it comes to words. I'm amazed her head doesn't explode.

Then she decided I should learn Kurdish! Seriously!?

'I teach!' she said.

'No!' I said.

'Yes!' she insisted.

'Why do I need to learn Kurdish?' I laughed. 'It's not like I'm ever going to go to . . .' I stopped because, of course, I didn't know where she was from. 'Er . . . your country,' I finished lamely. Then I asked, 'Actually, Nadima, where *do* you come from?'

She shook her head. I thought that maybe she hadn't understood me. So I tried asking her slowly and in a different way. 'Where – was – your – home?' But she shrugged and shook her head again. I gave up.

So we played 'What is please?' with the *entire* contents of my room – but *in Kurdish* – and with a new twist. By which I mean that each time I tried to repeat the Kurdish word for something, Nadima fell about laughing. Huh! Some friend!

Then Mum called up the stairs to say supper was ready.

Cue *chaos* in the kitchen. As usual The Brothers rushed in like a herd of stampeding rhinos (but with much longer legs and no horns of course). Gus sat down first, completely blocking Matt's way.

'Shift!' ordered Matt, shoving him to one side and clambering over him to get to his place. Dan, as usual, took a shortcut under the table to get to his chair.

'Oh!' cried Nadima in surprise as he scrambled out next to her.

'Excuse me!' he said cheerfully, before plonking himself down in his seat.

Mum ignored the mayhem, but Nadima looked

appalled! I cringed. They obviously had much better manners in their house.

'Hope you like pizza,' said Mum, putting several large ones onto the table.

'Mmmm. Pizza, yes!' beamed Nadima.

You know, it's really weird which English words Nadima knew. Except 'pizza' is Italian, now I come to think of it. Or is it American? Who knows?

Mum was *determined* we should talk to Nadima.

'Nadima, meet Dan, Gus and Matt,' she said, pointing at The Brothers.

Nadima did a funny little panicking grimace. I'm not surprised. The boys all look very similar. Even people who know us well, like Lil's parents, get them mixed up.

So then I had the brilliant idea of writing their names on Post-it notes and sticking them on their foreheads (a bit like that game where you have to guess which famous person you're meant to be).

So naturally the boys thought it would be *hilarious* to swap them around.

Gus put Matt's Post-it note on Dan and Dan's onto Matt.

'Oi, that's mine,' cried Matt, whipping the note off Gus's forehead and sticking it on his own.

'No, this one's yours, Matt!' said Gus, sticking Dan's note back on Matt.

Nadima looked completely bewildered.

'No, that's *mine*,' said Dan, snatching Gus's name off Matt's head.

By now they were all wearing the wrong name. 'This isn't helping!' I wailed.

Mum rolled her eyes. 'Guys! Give the girl a chance!' she begged.

But then Dan grabbed the pad of Post-its, wrote 'Idiot' and stuck it on my forehead.

'Hey!' I snatched the pad back and stuck 'dorkbrain' on his. Or rather I thought I had.

'What's a "drokbran"!?' snorted Dan.

'Not funny, Dan,' warned Mum with a look.

'You're right, Mum,' agreed Gus. 'Drokbran's not funny at all. But "Poopenfarter" is!'

Dan snorted with laughter.

'Oh, how very mature!' I said.

Mum looked at Nadima and rolled her eyes. 'Boys, huh!' she said.

'Yes! Boys, huh!' Nadima grinned. Mum shot me a surprised look and then burst out laughing.

'I taught her that!' I cried. 'It was on the very first day we met!'

73

'It'll probably come in very handy!' Mum laughed.

Cue howls of protest from The Brothers.

Nadima just sat there grinning away. She was obviously dead pleased with herself for making a joke.

When things had calmed down, Mum turned to Nadima and asked, 'So, where are you from?'

Nadima stopped smiling and frowned slightly. She didn't answer. So Gus grabbed the computer from the end of the table, and opened up a map of the world.

He was trying to be helpful.

15

Nadima's Home

'We live here, in England,' he said clearly, pointing at Britain on the screen. 'Where . . . did . . . you . . . live?' he asked slowly, and he nudged the computer nearer to her. We all looked at Nadima expectantly. I was pretty sure she'd understood. She stared at the map, blinked a couple of times and swallowed hard.

It suddenly hit me that maybe she didn't want to tell us. But then she pointed to the map and said, 'Syria.'

Syria.

It was like someone had chucked a bucket of cold water over everyone. I've never known it so quiet round the kitchen table in our house. You could have heard a pin drop.

'Syria?' repeated Mum, trying to sound all light-hearted and interested, rather than shocked.

But Nadima's face had gone all tight and she seemed close to tears.

I'd seen the pictures from Syria on the news. Well, we all have, haven't we? The smashed-up buildings and all those injured and dead people. Even little kids. It looked terrible. It *was* terrible. But up until that point I don't think I'd properly understood that it was happening to real people. But it was. Real people like Nadima.

I didn't know what to say. None of us did. Then Mum said gently to Nadima, 'It looks bad over there.'

Nadima looked down at her plate.

Mum waited to see if Nadima was going to say anything. But she just sat there with her eyes lowered.

'Well, we're glad you're here. Safe,' said Mum, breaking the horribly uncomfortable silence. And then she added, 'Perhaps you girls would like to eat in Jaz's room,' and she put some pizza slices on a plate and handed it to me.

I took Nadima's hand and gently pulled her up from the table.

'Drinks!' said Mum, holding out our glasses. Nadima took them, gave Mum a polite nod and followed me upstairs.

'Are you all right?' I asked, shutting my door.

Nadima didn't answer. So I didn't press her.

We sat on the floor, with our backs against my bed, and ate our pizza.

After a while I said, 'Was it very bad, back home? In Syria.'

She nodded.

'What was it like?'

She shrugged and shook her head.

I *think* she understood. But she didn't want to talk about it.

So we didn't say anything for a while. But it wasn't an awkward silence. We just sat together, munching our pizza and swigging our Cokes. I started wondering about how Nadima and her family had actually got here, all the way from Syria. The news was full of pictures of refugees on boats or hiding in lorries, or walking for days on end.

So after a while I said, 'How did you get here? To England?' I wasn't being nosy. At least I don't think I was.

But she shook her head again.

So I left it.

Maybe the journey had been so bad she didn't want to think about it, I thought. And then a really horrible idea struck me. What if something terrible had happened? I looked across at her. She seemed OK, just calmly eating her pizza, but I had absolutely no idea what she was thinking about, did I?

16

Death by Shopping!

The next morning I kept thinking about Nadima. It had been a bit of a shock, finding out where she came from, and it was weird being the only one who knew. I wondered whether I could talk to Lily about it. She was coming round early so we could go shopping for the camp-out – and the *compulsory* midnight feast of course. We were going to spend most of the day together – just us.

It had been *ages* since Lil and I had done *anything* together. I was so looking forward to it. I was a bit worried she might be funny with me for (*accidentally on purpose*) leaving Kara out. I bet Kara had been going on and on about it. But why shouldn't I invite Lil to something without Kara? Lily was my mate long before Kara even met her. And Kara and Lily did plenty of stuff without me. They never thought twice about leaving me out – did they?

I never left people out deliberately. Well, not usually. I thought of Nadima again – and felt rotten. I should have invited her to the camp-out. It *was* mean of me to leave her out just so that I could have a better time without her. *Really* mean of me. I remembered how she'd gone all quiet when Mum had asked where she came from, and how she hadn't wanted to talk about what it had been like. It must have been terrible. Really, really terrible. I should be trying to make things better for her, being extra nice to her. Not leaving her out.

Lil's mum and dad arrived to drop her off and have a 'quick' coffee with Mum. I ran down to the kitchen to say hi. Lily's dad swept me into a huge hug like he always does. Other kid's mums hug me all the time – but he's the only dad that hugs me. But then I've known him *forever*.

'We haven't seen you for ages!' cried Lil's mum. 'What have you been up to?'

'Growing, by the look of it!' laughed her dad.

I absolutely LOVE Lil's mum and dad. They're really funny and they do *everything* together. It's probably because they don't have any other kids to look after – so everything revolves around Lily.

'I hear there's a midnight feast planned for later,'

said Lily's dad, hoicking a ten-pound note out of his wallet. 'Do you need some money for carrot sticks, health bars and fruit?' he asked, with a perfectly straight face.

'No, but we do need some for marshmallows, chocolate and crisps!' declared Lily, snatching it out of his hand.

'Thank you!' I yelled as we ran up to my room to get ready to go shopping.

They were all still in the kitchen, nattering away, when Lily and I headed off into town. It was lovely – just like it used to be.

Lil and I stood at the self-service tills at the express supermarket in town checking we had everything.

'Marshmallows?' asked Lily.

'Check!'

'Crisps?'

'Check!'

'Cans of Coke?'

'Check!'

'Bag of popcorn?'

'Check!'

'Chocolate?'

'Double check!' I laughed, since we'd got *two*

bars. Cookies and cream (Lily's favourite) and caramel (my favourite).

'Sorted!'

We loaded the food into plastic bags and headed off to look around the clothes stores. Partly because we needed to get a birthday present for Chloe, but mostly because we just like looking at clothes. Lily and I are always swapping clothes – like sisters probably do. We know *exactly* what we both like. So we kept finding stuff that would be perfect for each other. We must've tried on about a hundred tops and skirts. We didn't actually buy anything of course – neither of us had any money!

I was really going to have to get my trading website up and running. I was fed up of being poor! I told Lil about it.

'OMG! That's a *brilliant* idea,' she said. 'I'd use it! I've got *loads* of stuff I could sell. Mum just takes it all to the charity shops!'

I literally *groaned*. 'Noooo! Don't let her take any more. Make her hang on to everything until we can sell it!'

Lily laughed. But by now we were tired and sticky, and the handles of the supermarket bags were cutting into my hands.

'Let's just get something for Chloe and go home,' I said.

'What d'you want to get her?' asked Lily.

Chloe's cat mad so I suggested a pink T-shirt we'd seen earlier, with a cat's nose and whiskers on it.

'OMG yes!' said Lily. 'She'd love it. Where was it?'

'I can't remember!' I groaned, and we both burst out laughing. She linked arms with me and we headed off to play Hunt-the-T-shirt! And then her phone rang. It was Kara.

'What's up?' Lily asked. She turned away from me and I heard her say, 'Shopping, with Jaz.'

You would think, wouldn't you, that Kara would take the hint and ring off? But no, she carried on talking to Lily for the best part of *half an hour* while Lily and I trudged back to all the shops we'd been to and I trawled through all the T-shirt rails until I found the cat one. Huh! I thought. So much for Kara having to devote *every precious moment* of the weekend to her dad.

It turned out the top was £19.99. Which was more than I could afford. So I just stood there, like a lemon, waiting for Lily to finish talking to Kara.

Eventually I pointed at my watch and pulled a face and Lily finally got the message.

'I've got to go, Kara. Yes, call you later,' she said and rang off. 'Kara's a bit upset,' she said, shoving her phone in her bag. 'She's had a row with her dad.'

I tried to be sympathetic. Actually, that's not true. I tried to *look* sympathetic. Then Lily noticed I'd found the T-shirt.

'Yes! That's perfect for Chloe!'

I pulled a face. 'I know, but I can't get it. It's too much!'

'How much too much?'

'£9.99 too much.'

'Let's get it together!' suggested Lily. 'It can be a joint present from both of us!'

We often used to do that, so I grinned and hugged her. On a scale of one to ten, I wondered how jealous Kara would be that Lil and I were giving Chloe a joint present. I guessed eleven.

As we walked back through town to get the bus home, one suddenly appeared round the corner – and we were still miles away from the stop!

'Lily! The bus!' I cried.

We pelted down the high street, our bags bashing

against our legs. We only just made it and literally *fell* onto the bus, gasping and laughing.

At which point Lily's phone rang – again. It was Kara – again.

'She's only calling you because she knows you're with me!' I said.

'No, she's not. I told you. She's upset. She's had a row with her dad!' she said, but she put her phone back in her pocket without answering it. Neither of us spoke for a while. After a bit she said, 'You know, Kara's actually really nice. You'd like her, if you got to know her.'

I do know her, and I don't like her, I thought. 'It's not that I don't like her,' I lied. 'It's just that she doesn't like me. And she doesn't like you being mates with me either.'

'Well, you don't like me being mates with her, do you?'

I shrugged.

'Look, I don't mind you being friends with Nadima,' said Lily.

'That's different. Nadima doesn't have any other friends. I'm just being nice. Trying to help her settle in. And there's nothing stopping you and me and Nadima all being friends.'

'Well, there's nothing stopping you and Kara and me all being friends either,' said Lily. 'Except you.'

'That's not fair!'

'Yes, it is! You've never liked her.'

I slumped back in my seat with my arms folded.

'All I'm saying is give her a chance,' she pleaded.

'Fine!' I said.

Lily sighed and looked out of the window. She knew I didn't really mean it. I tried to catch her eye, but she ignored me and kept staring out of the window.

So I leaned forward and said, 'I will, Lil, honest I will,' and I wasn't just saying it this time. I was going to try to be nice to Kara – for Lily's sake.

She turned and smiled at me. 'Thanks, Jaz.' I think it was more of a relieved smile than a happy one. But at least things felt a bit better again between us.

17

Camp-out

By the time we got home, Gus and Dan were in the back garden, putting our old blue tent up. It's huge – with a double sleeping section on each side and a sort of living area in the middle. Lil and I stashed our sleeping bags and pillows on one side, chucked the bags of food in after them and then went to grab all the cushions from the living-room sofa to dump in the middle bit. After that we strung the outdoor Christmas fairy lights along the fence and put tea lights in jam jars on the garden table.

It was going to be *magical* after dark.

Matt was piling up a *ridonkulously* huge mountain of burgers and sausages on the patio table next to the barbecue.

'Want a hand?' Lily asked him.

'Back off. This is Man Food!' joked Matt, pretending to threaten her with the big barbecue tongs.

Lily squealed and ducked out of range. She loves it when The Brothers tease her.

Chloe and Elly arrived just in time to eat, so we took our burgers and hot dogs into the tent. Then we lay on the cushions and watched the sky darkening. We'd lit the tea lights, and switched the fairy lights on, but it was still too light to really see them.

I kept expecting Kara to phone Lily. She didn't. But it didn't stop me worrying that she might. In the end (rather brilliantly, I thought), I suggested we all switch off our phones and talk instead. We talked about everything and anything – after a while we started talking about Nadima.

'What's she like?' asked Chloe.

'She's nice,' I said.

'How can you tell?' asked Elly. 'I mean, I don't want to be horrible or anything, but she hardly says anything.'

'I've hardly even spoken to her,' said Chloe. 'It's not that I don't want to. I just don't know what to say.'

'But she's just like us!' I said. 'You can talk about any old stuff.'

'Like what? I don't know anything about her,' said Lily.

'What bands does she like?' asked Chloe.

'Has she got any brothers or sisters?' added Elly.

'What does she like doing?' asked Lily.

I realised again that I didn't know very much about Nadima at all.

I knew where she came from, of course. Syria. But somehow it didn't feel right to tell the others – not even Lily. Nadima hadn't exactly been keen to tell me, had she? So maybe I should leave it up to her to tell people about her past.

'Does she have to wear that headscarf all the time?' Chloe asked suddenly.

'I don't know!' I cried. 'I'm not the world expert on headscarves!'

'Well, did she wear it yesterday when she came round to yours?' asked Elly.

'Yes . . .' I said.

'Maybe she does then.' Lily shrugged.

'Or maybe only when there are boys around,' suggested Elly.

'Do you think she'll wear it to my party?' asked Chloe.

'Probably!' I said. 'Honestly, why are you making such a fuss about a headscarf!'

'We're not! It's just that we don't wear one and she does,' said Elly.

'So? That doesn't make her different from us,' I said.

'We didn't say it did,' said Lily.

'Well, maybe we should think about what makes her the same as us rather than what makes us different!' I suggested. Which came out a lot snottier than I meant it to and Lily raised her eyebrows at me.

Then Chloe said, 'I hope she'll be all right at the cinema.'

'Why wouldn't she be?' I asked.

'Well, it's a bit of a responsibility, isn't it? With her not speaking English,' said Lily.

'Yeah, what if there's an emergency?' said Elly.

I roared with laughter. 'Elly, we're going to the movies, not free-fall parachuting! What's to worry about!? A massive popcorn explosion? Or maybe there'll be a violent volcanic eruption from the slushy machine!

We all collapsed laughing. Partly because it was funny, but also to relieve the tension filling the tent.

But actually I *was* anxious. What if something *did* happen at the cinema? A fire or something. Nadima wouldn't be able to understand what was going on and I wouldn't be able to explain it to her, or tell her what to do. I mean, I know she's not 'my responsibility'. But now that I knew more about her, I sort of felt I needed to look out for her a bit.

And then of course I started to feel bad again that I hadn't invited her to the camp-out. I could still have spent all day shopping with Lily. Nadima would have loved being here with us. I could imagine her lying in the tent, grinning away and trying to follow what was going on. Then she'd try to join in and we'd all fall about laughing – including her – when she said something wrong. But instead of that I'd left her out and she was probably sitting at home feeling lonely and miserable.

Pretty rubbish friend I was turning out to be.

18

Death by Maths!

Nadima greeted me with her usual big grin when I walked into our form room on Monday. I was worried that she might have heard about the camp-out from the others and she might be upset.

But she only said, 'Good morning, Jaz. Thank you for inviting me to your house on Friday. I had a really good time.'

It was another one of those funny little speeches she teaches herself. So I grinned at her and replied formally, 'You are very welcome, Nadima. Thank you for coming.' And then I crossed my fingers and hoped nobody mentioned the camp-out – especially Kara. I didn't think she'd miss a chance to stir things up. But I needn't have worried. She was far too busy telling everyone about her *terrible* weekend. We got a blow-by-blow account of her row with her dad. She sat perched on the table, flicking her hair dramatically, with the others clustered round her.

'It was awful!' she moaned. 'We were looking for a movie to watch online and I picked one but it was a 15 so he said I wasn't old enough.

But I told him I'd already seen it – and he hit the roof! He wanted to know who'd given me permission to watch it. So I said Mum had, and he demanded to know if she'd watched it with me. So of course I had to say no, because I watch movies in my room rather than the living room because of the little ones. And he lost his temper and said Mum was putting her stepkids before me and he rang her up and screamed down the phone at her.'

Kara held out her arms, signalling she needed a hug from Lily.

'Oh, Kara, that sounds dreadful,' said Lily, putting her arm round her.

Chloe and Elly hovered, making sympathetic faces.

'I hate my life,' Kara wailed melodramatically.

I was speechless. Honestly, Kara's melodramas are *pathetic* compared to what Nadima must have gone through in Syria. They're nothing! And Nadima doesn't go round saying how rubbish her life is and sobbing all over everyone. But I'd promised Lily I'd be nice – so I didn't even roll my eyes. I just tried to look sympathetic. Fyi, it nearly killed me.

Anyhow, by the time Kara had finished her sob story, Mrs W had arrived – and promptly ruined everyone's day.

'Right, 7R,' she announced, 'as I'm sure you've all remembered, and are looking forward to it with *wild* enthusiasm, it's the inter-form Maths Challenge this morning.'

Cue mass groans. We *had* all forgotten. I can't imagine how. It was clearly going to be the highlight of the term – like *The X Factor* meets *The Great British Bake Off*. Only with more maths, no excitement and no cakes.

'When the bell goes, make your way to the hall. You'll need your pencil cases and calculators!' she said.

A sea of hands shot up. 'Miss! I haven't got my calculator!' cried about half the class.

'Oh, bad luck!' Mrs W laughed. 'In that case you'll have to use your brains instead.'

Cue even more groaning.

*

Oh, how absolutely brilliant – death by maths.

Seriously, there ought to be a law against it.

The whole of Year 7 dawdled into the hall as slowly as humanly possible. Honestly, I've seen speedier snails. We had to put ourselves in groups of four and find a table to sit at. Of course Kara and Lily immediately paired up with Elly and Chloe, leaving Nadima and me out. So we teamed up with Ryan and Liam. I'm actually pretty good at maths. Which is handy – given that I'm going to be a *massively* successful millionaire business-woman with *loads* of money to deal with!

Ryan and Liam would be the first to admit they're not exactly maths geniuses. Class clowns, yes. Maths experts, no.

So I sighed, pulled the worksheet towards me and started to work through the questions. They weren't actually that hard. Nadima watched me and then suddenly pointed at the paper and said, 'No, Jaz, here is twenty-one. Is no eighteen.'

Then she took the pen off me and calmly did the sum again. And guess what, she was right!

Turns out Nad is *brilliant* at maths. At end of the challenge, we got full marks.

I'm just going to repeat that: *We Got Full Marks!*

Which was a school record! Not bragging, just saying. (Well, bragging really.) When we went up to get our medals, I tried not to shoot Kara a triumphant look. Honestly, I did try. Just not very hard. Nadima was thrilled to bits. She kept saying, 'Me happy, Mum be happy, Dad be happy!' And she didn't stop grinning all day!

Mind you, I was pretty made up too. I couldn't wait to tell Mum. And I was really pleased that I'd helped make something good happen to Nadima – for a change.

The Brothers teased me rotten about the medal. When Mum got home Matt took her to one side and said, with a perfectly straight face, 'You might need to have a little chat with Jaz. I think she's stolen someone's medal.'

'I didn't!' I laughed. 'I won it in the Maths Challenge.'

At which point Dan and Gus broke out into mock hysterical laughter.

Honestly! What are they like? It's a miracle I've got any self-confidence left *at all*.

'Pack it in, boys!' said Mum, giving me a huge hug. 'Well done, sweetheart!' she said, then added, 'Remind me, boys – has anyone in this house ever won a maths medal before?' Knowing full well no one had. Again, not bragging, just saying!

Then she hung my medal across the corner of the hall mirror with all the The Brothers' sports ones. It looked goooood!

After our *brilliant* success at the Maths Challenge, I think Nadima's parents must have decided I was a good influence on her or something. Because later that evening, she texted me:

Friday
My house

I texted back:

LOL.

19
Nadima's Family

Walking up the path with Nad to her front door, I suddenly felt nervous. Stupid really. I never normally worry about meeting new people. But I had no idea how much English her family could actually speak. And I didn't speak any Kurdish *at all*. What if we just sat there staring at each other all evening? How embarrassing would *THAT* be?

The front door opened. A woman stood in the doorway beaming at me. 'Hel-lo, hel-lo! Welcome, to my home!' she cried in a very strong accent. It was Nadima's mum (obviously). A small girl stood next to her, smiling at me shyly. And then a *very* little boy peered out from behind his mum's legs, and stared at me anxiously. He had the most enormous dark brown eyes – like pools of melted dark chocolate – and the longest lashes I have ever seen. He was so cute!

(Btw, why did I have to get three enormous great big brothers when little ones are so much cuter? *So* not fair!)

'This is my mother,' said Nadima. 'This is my sister. She is called Rasha. And this is my brother. He is called Sami.' It sounded like she was saying those phrases you learn in French in Year 6.

I smiled at them, but Sami ducked behind his mum, who laughed and tousled his hair. Then Nadima grabbed my hand and pulled me indoors.

I don't know what I was expecting. Cushions on the floor, low tables, Persian carpets and lots of those patterned metal lamps, I suppose. (I have obviously seen way too many Disney cartoons.) I wasn't expecting it to be like an ordinary house, with a dining table and chairs, a couple of sofas and a TV. But it was.

We followed Nadima's mum into the kitchen. There was a pan steaming away on the hob.

'Is Turkish Delight. I make for you!' she said, giving me a warm smile.

Nadima's mum was actually making Turkish Delight.

How awesome was *THAT*?

'Thank you! I love your Turkish Delight!' I said, and Nadima's face lit up as she grinned at me.

I looked around the kitchen. It was *plastered* with sticky labels. Everything in sight was labelled – *in English!*

Fridge . . . cooker . . . kettle . . . sink . . . tap . . . cupboard . . . drawer . . . There was even one on the ceiling!

Nadima's mother followed my gaze. 'Nadima do,' she said proudly. 'We *all* learning English.'

Then she turned back to the saucepan, picked up a bag of sugar and poured it in.

'What is called?' said Nadima. I thought she was asking me, as usual, but Rasha answered.

'Sugar!' she said.

'Yes! Good, Rasha!' said Nadima.

'Sugar!' repeated Nadima's mum, and then she spoke to Sami in Kurdish and they all looked at him.

Nadima knelt down next to him. 'Sami, say "sugar"!' she coaxed gently. He pulled his plump little mouth into a pout and said, 'Shu-da!'

OMG! Death by cuteness, or what?!

'Clever boy, Sami!' I laughed.

Nadima's mum smiled warmly and went back

to cooking the Turkish Delight. She picked up a packet, took out something that looked a bit like lasagne sheets and slid them into the pan, where they instantly melted away.

'What's that?' I asked Nadima. Shrugging, she handed me the packet.

It was written in English. But I couldn't actually read it, because the writing was fancy and squiggly and I really struggle when they do that.

'What is called?' Nadima asked me.

They all looked at me expectantly.

'Um . . .' I stalled. There was *no way* I was going to admit I couldn't read the label, so, rather ingeniously, if I say so myself, I said, 'Packet!' To be fair, the box was empty. So technically I *was* only holding a packet.

'Pack-et?' repeated her mum, looking at me questioningly.

Nadima shot me an odd look. And I knew, I just knew, she'd guessed I couldn't read the label. But she took the box out of my hand and held it up to her mum. 'Packet,' she said, and then she pointed at a couple of other cardboard boxes on the table and said, 'Packet . . . packet. Is right, Jaz? Yes?'

I wanted to hug her, but I just said, 'Yes!' and

101

then I went through everything on the table, pointing and saying, 'Packet, packet, bottle, bag, packet . . .' depending on the container.

'Ah!' said her mum. 'Thank you!'

Nadima took me upstairs to her room, which she shared with Rasha. We clambered up onto the top bunk. Rasha climbed up too, and then Sami wanted to join us. So we hauled him up by his dungarees. He was clutching a picture book, which he thrust at me. Then he confidently snuggled onto my lap, waiting for me to read it.

I hate reading aloud. It was only a picture book – and it's not like I couldn't read it. But it always feels like a test. So then I panic and muddle the words. I opened the book, but I could feel my face starting to go all hot. Nadima leaned over and took the book out of my hands.

'Is OK, Jaz. I read,' she said.

I shot her a grateful grin. I don't know how, but Nadima just . . . understood. I didn't even have to try to explain.

Which, given that it would probably be totally *impossible* to do that, was just as well!

20

Spas Dikum

A most amazing smell was drifting up to Nadima's bedroom – sort of spicy and sweet. By the time her mum called us down to eat, Nadima's dad had got home and was sitting at the table. He was wearing an old pair of jeans and a tatty sweatshirt. He wasn't old, but what I noticed most about him was the grey, almost white, hairs in his dark beard and the wrinkles round his eyes. He seemed nice, but meeting people's dads always makes me a bit nervous. Probably because I haven't got one.

'Hel-lo. I am Nadima father,' he said slowly and in a very thick accent.

'I am Jaz, hello,' I said, just as slowly.

He nodded and smiled at me. I wasn't sure whether to try to say anything else – I didn't know how much English he knew and I didn't want to embarrass him. So we just sat there.

There was a bit of an uncomfortable silence, but fortunately her mum soon came in with the food on a big round dish. It was some sort of spicy lamb stew, on a bed of yellow rice, with roasted almonds sprinkled on the top and slices of lemons around the edge. It looked *fabulous* and smelled even better. Her mum had obviously gone to a *huge* amount of trouble to make me something really special. I cringed when I remembered the pizzas we'd given Nadima at ours.

'What is it?' I asked Nadima.

'Is *mansaf*,' she replied. 'Is lamb.'

'Mmm, I love lamb!' I cried.

Her mum handed me a plateful and I took a forkful.

'Is good? Yes?' she asked anxiously.

'Yes, yes! It's delicious!' I mumbled with my mouth full, and she beamed at me.

Then Rasha and Sami started jabbering away in Kurdish, and soon the rest of the family joined in and, even though I couldn't understand a word of it, it was much better than us all sitting there in total silence.

So I just kept eating and smiling. I smiled so much I thought my face would get stuck. Nadima translated as much as she could – which wasn't much.

Then she tried to teach me to say '*spas dikum*' which means 'thank you' in Kurdish.

I had a go, and both her parents smiled at me. Nadima and Rasha, on the other hand, fell about laughing. Huh!

After we'd eaten, we all sat in the living room and her parents tried to talk to me. I think they'd learned some sentences specially. Which was really lovely of them, when you think about it.

'In Syria, we have sweet shop,' announced her dad proudly.

'I make lots of sweets,' said her mum. 'I show you.' Picking up their laptop she showed me some photos of Syrian sweets for sale in a market.

And OMG they looked *amazing*. Like those little sweet sticky pastries you get in Greek restaurants, and all piled up in towering pyramids. Nadima's mum pointed at them and rattled off a list of names. I couldn't keep up.

Then Nadima pointed at one. 'I like best. Is baklava.'

'Baklava! I've had baklava!' I said.

'Ah!' they all cried together, and burst out clapping!

I've never been applauded for eating sweets before! It was a crazy moment. Crazy, but lovely.

Then Nadima tried to teach Sami to say 'Jaz' – but he was too shy.

When Matt came to pick me up, Nadima's mum handed me a plastic tub with the Turkish Delight she'd made. It was still a bit gloopy, and she said something to Nadima.

Nadima took out her phone, typed for few seconds and then showed me the screen.

> Eat it tomorrow.

'OK!' I nodded. Then I added, *'Spas dikum!'* I wished I'd thought to learn how to say 'Goodbye' in Kurdish too.

As we drove along the street, I looked at the other houses, and I remember thinking it was weird. They were ordinary people, living in an ordinary house in an ordinary street – like everyone else. But they weren't just like everyone else, were they? Her story wasn't just ordinary, was it? And nobody knew.

21

Turkish Delish!

As soon as we got home The Brothers buzzed round the Turkish Delight like bees round a honey pot.

'It's not set!' I cried, shoving them away. I put it on the side in the kitchen. 'We can have it tomorrow!'

Then I told them about how Nadima's family had had their own sweet shop.

'Their own sweet shop! Now *that's* the kind of parents I want!' said Gus.

'Yeah,' agreed Dan. 'How come we get a crummy estate agent for a parent, and they get their own sweet shop?' he teased.

'Bad luck!' Mum grinned.

'Yeah, well, they haven't got it
quietly.

Mum sighed. 'I can't ever
hard it must be to leave
you love,' she said. 'A

where you're not at all sure of your welcome – I'm ashamed of how few refugees we've taken in.'

'I reckon everyone should have the right to live wherever they want to,' I said.

'It's not that simple,' said Matt. 'There are millions of refugees.'

'We can't take all of them,' said Dan.

'No one country could take all of them,' added Matt.

'But they don't all want to come to the UK, do they?' I argued.

'A lot of them do,' said Mum. 'And to be fair, we don't have enough housing for all of them.'

'Then we should build some more,' I said.

'But it takes ages to build houses. Where would they live in the meantime?' asked Dan.

'Tents!' replied Gus.

'What about when it snows?!' I cried. 'They'd freeze to death.'

'OK, so would you give up your bedroom for a refugee to live in?' Dan asked me.

'No, I'd give up yours!' I told him.

He thwacked me with a cushion.

*

The next morning was Saturday so I'd gone down early to grab the computer, as usual. While it was loading, I checked if the Turkish Delight had set. It had – so I cut it into chunks with a sharp knife and turned it out onto a plate. Obviously I had to try a bit. And OMG it was amazing. I don't know how I resisted scoffing the lot. Actually I do. It was knowing what The Brothers would do to me if I did.

Not surprisingly, we polished off all the Turkish Delight before breakfast. And then World War Three nearly broke out over the last piece, so Mum made us bid for it. Matt won with a 50p bid. Mum put the money in the treats pot in the kitchen cupboard.

And I had a *brilliant* new business idea.

Fifty pence for ONE piece of Turkish Delight? Seriously?! What if we got Nadima's mum to make tons of it and we sold it at school?

We'd make a fortune!

Entrepreneurial or what!?

I wondered if Nadima would be up for it. But then I thought that actually it would be great – because she'd sort of be getting a part of her old life back. And it'd give her a chance to show everyone what her family had done, back in Syria.

I was itching to tell Nadima my *fabulous* plan. I thought about texting her, but I realised it would be almost as difficult for me to *write* the text as it would be for her to *read* it. By which I mean *impossible*. It would have to wait until I could explain everything at school next week.

22
Movie

On the Sunday afternoon we all met up at the cinema for Chloe's party. The others were already there collecting the tickets by the time Matt dropped me off. Nadima hadn't shown up yet, but there was still loads of time before the movie, so I wasn't worried.

I handed Chloe her present. 'It's from me and Lily,' I said. 'We chose it together.'

Chloe ripped off the paper, pulled out the T-shirt and held it up. 'OMG I love it!' she cried. 'Thank you!' Lily and I grinned at each other.

I glanced over to catch Kara's reaction. I thought she'd be jealous, but she was too busy grabbing centre stage for that.

'Ooooh!' She snatched the T-shirt off Chloe and held it up against herself. 'I want one!'

There was still no sign of Nadima. I was beginning to get anxious.

'I wonder if she's going to come,' said Elly.

'Maybe she felt a bit shy,' said Lily.

'What if she doesn't know where the cinema is?' said Chloe.

'She'll look it up on her phone, like we would!' I laughed, but actually I *was* properly worried by now. What if she'd got lost? I should have offered to give her a lift.

'I'll call her,' I said. But just as I was digging my phone out of my pocket Nadima came rushing through the doors.

'I sorry. I sorry!' she panted. 'I get off bus. Is wrong stop! I run!'

'It's fine!' I said. 'Don't worry!'

I *literally* can't tell you how relieved I was.

Nadima handed Chloe a small colourful paper bag. 'Happy Birthday,' she said.

'Thank you!' said Chloe, opening the bag. She took out a bright yellow bath bomb and looked at the label. '"Lemon Sherbet Fizz-Bomb"!' she read.

Nad looked confused. 'No! Is not bomb! Is for bath!' she said, and everyone burst out laughing.

'They are called "bath bombs"!' I told her.

'Ahhh!' She nodded then rolled her eyes

exaggeratedly at her mistake and repeated, '*Bath bombs.*'

'Come on,' said Kara. 'I need to check my make-up,' and she headed off to the loos. So of course we all trooped after her, and the others all started touching up their make-up too. It was *ridonkulous*! We were going to be sitting in a dark cinema – so who was going to see them? Nadima and I just stood and watched. I'm sure she was thinking the same as me.

Lily held out her make-up bag to Nadima. 'Do you want to borrow some mascara or some lipstick?' she asked, slowly.

Nadima shook her head.

'Maybe she's not allowed to wear any,' said Elly.

'Nadima and I don't need any make-up,' I announced solemnly. 'We're already stunning enough,' and I started doing some poses in the full-length wall mirror. Nadima copied me and we strutted and pouted like supermodels. 'Somebody call *Vogue*!' I said, and everyone laughed.

'Do you have to wear that?' asked Kara, pointing at Nadima's headscarf. 'You can take it off here, if you want. We won't tell,' she added, and she mimed taking off a headscarf.

I was a bit worried because I didn't want Nadima to get into trouble, or feel awkward. But she just grinned at Kara and shook her head. 'I like,' she said.

Kara shrugged and went back to plastering her eyelashes with mascara. I was beginning to realise how strong Nad was. Way too strong to be pushed around by Kara, that was for sure. *Finally* everyone was ready so we got some popcorn and went in.

I have absolutely *no idea* how much of the movie Nadima understood. But it looked like she was having fun. She laughed out loud a couple of times and she *definitely* got it when the lousy two-timing boy cheated on his girlfriend and went on a date with another girl. But of course that might have been because all the girls in the audience booed and hissed at him! LOL.

When we were back in the foyer she tapped Chloe on the arm, took a deep breath and said, 'Thank you for inviting me to you birthday party. It is very kind of you. You are very nice. I hope you have good birthday.'

I could see Chloe was really impressed and pleased by Nadima's little speech. But Nadima hadn't finished.

'Now I sing "Happy Birthday to You"!' she announced.

We were gobsmacked!

'Seriously?!' I cried.

She nodded and grinned. 'Is from YouTube!'

Then she started off singing on her own (which must've taken huge guts, when you come to think of it) so we all joined in. Everybody in the cinema was looking at us, but we didn't care. And I'm telling you, WE WERE AWESOME! Especially when Kara went and sang *in harmony*. We sounded like a proper group.

It was typical of Kara to show off, I thought, but for Lily's sake I said, 'You have a fab voice, Kara!'

'Thank you!' she replied, then she grabbed Lily's arm. 'Hey, we should form a girl band!' she cried, and she linked arms with me and Lily, so I linked up with Nadima, and Elly and Chloe tacked themselves onto the end next to her. And we all did a swanky walk out of the cinema like we were shooting a music video or something. Everyone stared at us. It was *brilliant*!

It was a fantastic afternoon, and everyone had had a real laugh. Why couldn't it be like this all the time?

23

Turkish Delight

We were all in a great mood on Monday morning before registration. Liam had borrowed one of Lily's hairbands and was carefully putting Ryan's hair up into a topknot. Ryan looked *ridonkulous*! But he took a quick selfie, looked at it critically and announced, 'I want bunches too,' so Chloe and Kara handed over their hairbands as well.

Then Elly got out her make-up. 'Let me do your lashes, Ryan!' She waggled her mascara at him.

'Nooooo!' yelped Ryan, leaping out of his seat.

Nadima and I were *killing* ourselves laughing.

So we were all too busy mucking about for me to get the chance to tell her about my *spectacular* Turkish Delight business plan before lessons.

The first lesson was drama (groan) and Nadima and I were meant to be coming up with ideas for our box story (double groan). So I got out my phone and tried to explain that to her.

I typed 'we mak up stroy' into my phone. Then I looked at the Kurdish translation.

English	Kurdish
we make up stroy	em hesabekî xwe stroy

Fyi, Kurdish must be the hardest language to read in the *entire* world. I showed the screen to Nadima, but she frowned and shook her head. 'I not understand.'

So I made it easier and just put 'stroy'

Which turned out to be:

English	Kurdish
stroy	ku hîsa

She shook her head again., Pointing at the screen, she said, 'What is "stroy"?'

'Stroy?' I said, confused. Then I looked at what I'd typed. Maybe I'd spelt story wrong. So I typed 'stroy' into a text and it autocorrected to 'story'.

'Doh!' I laughed, face-palmed and corrected my mistake.

English	Kurdish
story	çîrok

'Ah! Yes!' She laughed, nodding.

English	Kurdish
we mak story	em hesabekî nûçeyê

So then I put 'we mak story' and got . . . and my heart sank. The Kurdish word 'çîrok', (which apparently means 'story') wasn't there. None of the words had a 'c' with a little squiggle under it followed by an 'i' wearing a hat thing, and a 'k' at the end. Even I could see that. So the Kurdish sentence couldn't be about making up a story at all.

'Yes, yes! I understand!' said Nadima.

I shook my head. 'No,' I said. 'No. You can't.'

'Yes, yes!' she insisted.

'Seriously, no, you don't.' I told her. She looked very confused.

So I gave up and decided to tell her about my brilliant Turkish Delight business instead. Well, *our* Turkish Delight business.

I opened my drama book and drew lots of little square chunks. 'Turkish Delight,' I said.

Then I added a picture of a stick person stirring a big saucepan. I wrote 'Nad' on the picture.

'You make Turkish Delight,' I said.

'OK.' She nodded.

Then I drew us standing at a table and labelled us 'Nad + Jaz' and added lots of Turkish Delight.

Then I drew a stick person holding a 50p piece, standing by the table. (I had thought about charging more, but I decided it would be good to make it cheaper than a bar of chocolate. See – good business thinking.)

Then I put an arrow from the coin to us, and another one from a bag Turkish Delight to the stick person.

'We sell Turkish Delight. Here at school,' I said.

It was the work of a genius, if I say so myself. Well, it must have been, because she immediately understood me.

'Yes! Yes!' She grinned. 'We sell Turkish Delight. We get money!'

'Yes!'

We were so engrossed we didn't notice Mrs P looming up to see how we were getting on. I didn't have time to shut my book. I froze and Nadima flicked me a quick look of panic. We both held our breaths as Mrs P scanned the drawing. But then she said, 'Brilliant, brilliant, girls! That looks like a *wonderful* story idea. Well done!'

I nearly exploded with laughter. As soon as Mrs P left, we both collapsed giggling.

When we'd recovered I said, 'Will your mum be OK? Making lots of Turkish Delight?'

'I make!' said Nadima, tapping herself. 'Not mum. Me!'

'Er . . . when?' I asked, wondering how she was going to make enough of the stuff. There's no point launching a product if you don't have plenty of stock. (See? That's why dyslexics make good businesspeople. We think about everything. It's called 'Big Picture Thinking'.)

'Tonight. I make three . . . er . . .' She mimed a square shape with her hands.

'Tins?' I suggested.

'Yes, three tins!'

'Oh, OK.'

While I was mentally working out how many chunks that would make, she said, 'And tomorrow – three tins!'

'Seriously? Six tins?' I asked. 'In two days?!'

'Huh!' she scoffed. 'Make Turkish Delight is easy-peasy, lemming squeezy!'

I burst out laughing.

Six tins would be plenty, I reckoned, so that meant we could sell it on Wednesday.

We were going to make a killing.

Except that on the day it didn't quite go to plan.

24

Disaster

On Wednesday morning Nadima walked into class with two *huge* tubs full of Turkish Delight. They were so big she couldn't even get them in her school bag. She'd had to use one of those extra-strong supermarket bags. As soon as she'd dumped them on our table, the nosey parkers of 7R were all over her like chocolate sprinkles on a strawberry trifle.

'Oooh, what's in there?' asked Liam, his eyes lighting up greedily.

I beckoned him closer. 'Can you keep a secret?' I asked.

He nodded eagerly.

'Well, so can I!'

'Bet it's something to eat,' said Ryan, making a grab for the bag.

'Oi! Hands off!' I gave him a friendly shove. 'You'll find out at break.'

Then Kara came over, followed by the others.

'Is it your birthday?' she asked Nadima casually.

'No. Is not birthday,' replied Nadima, confused.

'She thinks it's birthday cake,' I explained slowly to Nadima with a grin.

'Ah,' said Nadima, nodding.

'I was right! It *is* cake!' cried Kara gleefully.

'No. Is not cake,' said Nadima flatly.

Kara's face was a picture. I bit my lip, trying not to laugh.

'Well, what is it then?' she demanded crossly.

'We'll tell you at break,' I said.

'Oh, come on!' begged Chloe.

'What's the big secret?' asked Lily.

'If I told you that, then it wouldn't be a secret, would it?' I replied, with impressive logic.

'Aren't we all a little bit big for secrets?' said Kara witheringly.

I just shrugged.

When the bell rang for break, Nad and I threw our books into our bags and literally *ran* to set up a table to sell our Turkish Delight. I'd chosen a *brilliant* spot – by the bench outside our form room. We quickly dragged a table outside. Then Nadima arranged the chunks of Turkish Delight in pyramids on the lids of the tubs. At first there were loads of kids all pushing and shoving to see what it was we were selling.

'What's *that*?!' asked some oik rudely.

'It's Turkish Delight!' I said, offering him a chunk. 'Try it!'

'No way! It looks weird!' he said.

'Yeah, like soap or something,' added his mate. Some of the kids laughed.

'But it tastes lovely – honest! I shoved a chunk into my mouth to prove it. 'Just try it. And it's cheaper than chocolate!' I added.

'I'm not surprised,' said someone else, obviously trying to be funny.

I glanced at Nadima. She looked really upset. I don't know how much she understood what they were saying – but it was pretty obvious from their faces what was going on. Nobody would even try it.

And then Kara and everyone turned up.

'So this is the big secret?' she said. 'Turkish Delight.'

'Yeah, want some? Only 50p a bag,' I said.

She shook her head. 'I can't stand it,' she said. 'It's all gooey.'

124

'But this isn't! It's home-made. It's not like the stuff you get in the shops.'

Kara wrinkled her nose – rudely, I thought.

'Lil?' I said, offering her a piece. She pulled a face. 'I've just had some crisps.'

By now Nadima's face was flushed and I could see she was either angry or trying not to cry – probably both.

I suddenly saw it from her point of view. It wasn't just bags of sweets the kids were dissing – it was her whole background. Back home in Syria her family did this for a living. But the kids in our school were literally *sneering* at her Turkish Delight. Honestly, how ignorant can you get? She was upset and I was *furious* – especially with Kara and Lily. How could they be so mean? It wouldn't have killed them to just *try* a piece, would it? Even if they were only doing it to be polite. Nadima was trying so hard to be friends with everyone, and then they turn round and are just downright rude to her.

It was a disaster. We didn't sell any. Not a single piece. We couldn't even give it away. I can't tell you how rubbish I felt.

And then, just when I thought things couldn't get any worse, guess what? It got worse.

125

25
Detention

Mr Y nosed over.

'Jaz Watson! What on earth do you think you're doing?' he spluttered. 'You can't sell things on school property. This is a school, not a street market! Pack it all up *immediately*, and then go straight to the head. Both of you.'

I didn't even bother to protest.

'We can't sell it!' I explained to Nadima as I started putting the bags back into the boxes.

'Why?' she asked.

I shrugged.

'Is trouble?' she asked anxiously, helping me to pack up.

'No. It'll be fine. Don't worry,' I said.

But I could tell by her expression she didn't believe me. She looked worried. Actually, she looked frightened.

We stood in front of Mrs C's desk. Nadima was scared stiff. I grabbed her hand and gave it a squeeze.

'Jaz Watson, you again!' said Mrs C, glaring at me over her glasses.

'But it's not my fault!' I protested. 'I didn't know we weren't allowed to sell Turkish Delight.'

'You're not allowed to sell *anything* on school property.' Mrs C sighed.

'Well, how was I supposed to know that? It's not like you hand us a list of all the rules when we get here. And anyhow, I bet the rules don't actually say we can't sell things.'

Mrs C raised her eyebrows. Looking back, I should have read the warning signs.

'They don't actually say you're not allowed to murder your maths teacher either – but everyone knows you're not.'

'But that's because murder is against the law, but selling stuff isn't!' I exclaimed.

'That's not the point, Jaz, and you know it. If you want to sell Turkish Delight, why not do it for Charity Challenge Week?'

(Because, I thought, that isn't going to make any money for us, is it? But I didn't say that, obviously.)

I shot Nadima a quick look. She was close to tears. But Mrs C hadn't finished. She paused before she dropped the bombshell.

I'm giving you both an after-school detention.'

'That's not fair! You can't punish us for doing something we didn't even know was wrong!' I cried.

'I have to. I can't let this go. It will signal to other children that they can sell things in school too. I have to set an example.'

Then she turned to Nadima and spoke slowly and clearly. 'You have to stay here, after school, today. Do you understand?'

Nadima's face crumpled and she burst into tears.

I begged Mrs C to let Nadima off. 'It wasn't her fault! It was all my idea,' I told her.

'You got Nadima into trouble and you'll both have to face the consequences.'

'That is so unfair!' I shouted, and stormed out of her office. Nadima followed me and then, as soon as we'd got away from Mrs C's office she started shouting at me! First in Kurdish and then in English. Well, bits of English.

'This bad. You bad. You bad friend. You get me trouble.'

'It's only a detention, Nadima!' I said.

'Is trouble! Trouble is bad. If I bad, maybe they send us back! Back to Syria.'

'They won't, Nad!' I cried. 'Nobody's going to send you back to Syria! They can't. Not just because you got a detention!' Honestly?! She was being ridiculous!

'YOU NOT KNOW. YOU NOT KNOW!' she yelled. 'Maybe we not safe now. And is your fault!'

She let rip a string of Kurdish words. I had no idea what they meant, but it was pretty clear what *she* meant. Then she turned on her heel and walked off.

26
Trouble

The school bus had gone ages ago, so now I was going to have to find my own way home.

Oh, how absolutely brilliant. Could this day get any better?

Detention had been horrible. Nadima wouldn't even sit next to me. I tried to talk to her, to say sorry, but she turned her back. And then, as soon as it was over, she grabbed her bags and walked off. The supermarket bag, still full of Turkish Delight, banged against her leg as she strode away.

So now I was either going to have to walk home, or call Mum, fess up to getting detention and ask her to come and fetch me.

It was a no-brainer.

I started walking. But then I heard a car horn honking. I turned round and there was Mum, parked in the drop-off area. One of the boys must have told her. I was in *sooo* much trouble.

Through the windscreen I could see her drumming her fingers on the steering wheel. I got in next to her.

'Well?' she asked, crunching the gears and shooting back in reverse.

'I got a detention.'

'So Matt told me. I had to cancel a house viewing and leave work early to come and pick you up. *And* I had to phone the school to find out when after-school detention finishes. Can you imagine how embarrassing that was?'

I didn't reply. I just stared out of the window. I didn't need a reminder that my after-school detention was a first in our house.

'Were you planning to tell me yourself?' she challenged.

'I thought you'd be angry.'

'Damn right!'

'But it wasn't my fault!' I wailed, and told her what had happened.

'So you got a detention for doing something you didn't know was wrong. Correct?' she said, calming down a bit.

'Yes!' I cried heatedly. 'It wasn't fair! I'm fed up of this *stupid* school and their *stupid* rules and *stupid, stupid* Mrs C.'

'Jaz – be honest with me. Was it what you did, or *how you spoke to Mrs C afterwards*, that got you into trouble? I know you. You go charging in like a bull in a china shop and you make things worse.'

'No! I didn't! I was perfectly polite!' I insisted, frantically going back over the conversation in my mind trying to remember what I had actually said.

'Well, in that case it does seem harsh, giving you a detention when you didn't know you were breaking the rules. Do you want me to call . . . ?' but I didn't let her finish.

'It's not that! That's not the problem,' I yelled, and promptly burst into tears.

Mum pulled over and tried to scoop me into a clumsy hug. It was a bit difficult because of the seat belts and because I'm a bit too big for scooping up these days. I hardly ever cry, but I just couldn't stop. Great big sobs and floods of tears until my face (and Mum's jumper) was smeared with snot.

'What is it, sweetie?' she asked, her face full of concern. 'What else happened?'

'I've got Nadima into trouble!' I wailed. 'Now *she's* angry with me and she doesn't want to be friends with me any more, and I doubt her family would let her even if she did! She called me a "bad friend". I'm not a bad friend. I'm not! I didn't know we would get into trouble. But I couldn't even explain that.'

Tears dribbled off my face and down my neck. Mum handed me a bit of folded-up kitchen towel from the pocket in the car door. I blew my nose, sniffed hard and carried on.

'I begged Mrs C not to give Nadima a detention. I *begged* her. I *told* her it wasn't her fault. But she said that if I'd got Nadima into trouble then I'd have to *"face the consequences"*. But it's not just ME *"facing the consequences"*, is it?' I raged. 'It's Nadima too! And she's *terrified* that if anyone in her family gets into any trouble they'll all be sent back to Syria.'

'Jaz! Calm down! They're not going to get deported just because Nadima got an after-school detention!' said Mum.

'I know that – but they don't, do they?'

'Sweetheart, we can sort this out. We can explain to Nadima's family,' Mum said soothingly.

'No, we can't! That's the whole problem. They don't speak English!'

'Come on, this isn't like you,' said Mum, and she sort of pushed me away so she could look at me. 'I'm sure we can find a way to deal with this.'

'No, Mum! We can't! It's not like I'm a little kid any more,' I shouted. 'You can't just make everything better with a hug or a sticking plaster and a bit of chocolate!'

Mum reeled back like I'd slapped her. 'OK. Well, let's just leave it then, shall we?' she said.

She wasn't expecting a reply, so I didn't give her one.

We drove in silence. When we got home I stomped up to my room and slammed the door. I didn't even bother to text Nadima. There was no point.

27
Hiding

When I woke up the next morning my stomach instantly went into knots and I felt sick. The whole scene with Nadima outside Mrs C's office came flooding back to me. There was absolutely no way I could face going into school. What if she still wasn't talking to me? And not only that, Kara would gloat her head off.

After a while I heard a message ping in. I grabbed my phone, hoping it was from Nadima. It wasn't. There were a few new texts, but none from her. I couldn't face getting up. I dropped my phone back on the floor and hunched down under the quilt.

When I wasn't down for breakfast Mum came up and put her head round my door. 'Come on! It's half seven!'

I rolled over to face the wall. 'I'm not going in today,' I said. 'I'm not well.'

She came over and sat on the bed.

'Is this about Nadima?'

'No!' I lied. 'I'm ill.'

Mum obviously didn't believe me, because she said, 'If you go in you'll be able to put things right with her.'

'No, I won't! She's not even speaking to me.'

She paused for a moment and then said, 'Jaz, these things often sort themselves out once everyone's had time to calm down.' I didn't say anything, so then she said, 'You don't think you might be overreacting a little?'

'No! I don't!' I cried. 'She said I was a "bad friend", and she's right. I'm a rubbish friend. Lily would rather be friends with Kara than me, and now I've messed everything up with Nadima and she doesn't want to be friends with me either.'

'No, you haven't, sweetie. She was worried and upset about getting a detention. Perhaps she was scared about how her parents would react.'

'And that's another thing! What if her parents won't let her be friends with me any more?'

Mum reached out and tucked a bit of stray hair behind my ear. Then she said, 'I honestly think you should get up and go in and try to sort things out. You can't run away like this.'

'I'm not running away! I told you, I'm ill. I've got a headache and I feel sick,' I cried.

She put her hand on my forehead. It felt lovely and soft and cool. It reminded me of when I was little.

'I really don't feel well,' I said, lying back on the pillow and shutting my eyes. I wasn't even acting. I didn't feel up to going to school. The more I thought about going in, the worse I felt.

'OK. Stay off today. I'll call and tell them you're sick,' said Mum.

'Thanks,' I said, rolling over and staring at the wall again.

'Do you want me to bring you some breakfast before we go?'

'No, thanks. I don't want anything,' I replied. I wasn't even pretending.

I didn't feel like doing anything all day. I couldn't even be bothered to work on my website or my business plan. I just lay in bed listening to music and watching stuff. You'd think bunking off would be fun – it wasn't. It was dead boring and I kept thinking about Nadima. And then I'd feel sick and anxious again.

All through the day I kept hearing texts pinging into my phone. I kept hoping there'd be one from Nadima. There wasn't. They were mostly from Lily. I didn't feel in the mood to answer them. But she kept on texting anyway. Which was nice of her.

Are you OK?
What's up?
Are you ill?

At lunchtime she must've gone to find one of The Brothers to see what was wrong with me because she texted:

Gus says you're sick.
Poor you.

Followed by:

Everyone says Hi and get well soon.

138

And then:

Will you be in tomorrow?

I thought about trying to skive off the next day too. But I knew Mum wouldn't let me. Not unless I *literally* threw up everywhere. Besides, if I didn't go in on Friday and sort things out, then Mum would probably make me go round to Nadima's over the weekend. That would be even worse – I'd have to face her mum and dad.

Mum was right. I couldn't run away from this forever.

So I texted Lil.

Much better
See you tomorrow
Jx

Tomorrow. I didn't even want to think about it.

The next morning I was desperate to get in early enough to catch Nadima so I could talk to her on her own – without everyone eagerly hanging around with their ears flapping. Fat chance. The Brothers didn't seem to understand the phrase 'Hurry up! We have to go! NOW!' It was like watching sloths race, the way they ambled to the car.

By the time I *finally* got into our form room Nadima was sitting between Kara and Lily, on their table.

When she saw me she blushed and looked away. She didn't even say hi. I guessed that meant she still wasn't talking to me. I was gutted. But I was determined not to show it, so I managed to smile at everyone.

'Are you feeling better?' Kara asked me, and I'm pretty sure she meant it sarcastically.

But I remembered I'd promised to be nice to her, for Lily's sake, so I just said. 'Much better, thank you.' Then I slid into my seat, hoping Nadima would join me. She didn't. Well, not until Mrs W came in for registration and by then it was a bit late to try to sort things out so I decided to leave it until break. And then the first lesson changed everything.

It was French. Much to my surprise, Lily sat down next to me. I looked round – Nadima was sitting next to Kara.

'Hope you don't mind,' said Lily. 'But when you

were off I swapped places with Nadima so she wouldn't have to sit on her own. And she seemed to get on really well with Kara helping her – so we thought we should carry on like it.'

I was speechless.

'You don't mind, do you? I thought you'd be pleased we were sitting together again,' she said.

'No, I am,' I mumbled. 'Course I am!' And I would have been. I *should* have been. But I couldn't stop feeling that Kara had done it again. Somehow she'd managed to steal another friend off me.

28
Sorry

As soon as I got home Mum asked if I'd managed to sort things out with Nadima.

'No,' I said.

She gave me one of her looks.

'I didn't get a chance!' I protested. 'She's sitting next to Kara now.'

'Oh!' she said, sounding surprised but trying not to react.

'And, well, there wasn't really a moment when it was just me and Nadima – and I didn't want to bring it up in front of everyone,' I said.

'Ah,' said Mum. Then after a moment she added, 'Well, we'll just have to have a think about what to do next,' and gave me a quick hug.

There was every danger I was going to cry, so I quickly slid off up to my room.

I sat on my bed and had a 'think about what to do next'.

Once I'd got past some lovely fantasies involving shoving Kara off a cliff, or into a swimming pool full of great white sharks, or into a pit of poisonous snakes, I realised I wasn't going to be able to rely on any of those wonderful scenarios and I'd have to sort it out for myself.

I went downstairs to the computer. Gus was on it.

'Are you going to be long?' I asked him.

'Hours,' he replied.

'In that case, can I just borrow it for a few minutes?'

'Nope!'

'Please!'

'Nope!'

'But it's really important!'

He paused and looked at me. 'Seriously?'

'Yes, seriously,' I said.

'OK. Ten minutes.'

I hugged him. 'Thanks, Gus.'

He sloped off upstairs, calling over his shoulder, 'Let me know if you need any help. AND LET ME KNOW WHEN YOU'RE DONE!'

I opened up a Word document. Which was a good start. But then I got stuck. I stared at the empty page. It's always like this when I have to write anything. My mind goes blank.

Fortunately, because I'm dyslexic, I have a *brilliant* strategy to deal with this. I just stop thinking about what I want to *write* and think about what I want to *say* instead. Sometimes I even imagine myself talking to someone.

I opened Google Translate, typed 'im sory' into the English box and clicked on Kurdish. I got this:

English	Kurdish
im sory	Sory im

I wasn't convinced. It looked suspiciously like what I'd written – only backwards – and there weren't any of those little squiggly marks and funny hat things that I'd seen all over Kurdish words.

Since it was a Friday, Mum had come into the kitchen to start cooking supper. She saw me staring blankly at the screen.

'You OK?' she asked.

'I'm typing a note to Jaz's family.'

She came and looked over my shoulder at what I'd typed.

'Ah,' she said, 'I detect a minor flaw in your otherwise excellent and fine, upstanding plan. You don't speak Kurdish . . . they don't speak English . . . and the computer doesn't speak Jaz!'

I laughed.

'Budge over,' said Mum. 'You talk, I'll type!'

So together we wrote a short note. The shorter the better, we thought.

English	Kurdish
we make up stroy got into trouble.	Ez xemgîn Nadima rabû nav belayê im.
I did not know it was against the rules to sell things in school.	Min bi xwe nizanibû ku ew li dijî qaîdeyên bû bo firotina tiştên di dibistanan de?
Please can I be Nadima's friend?	

(See? Loads of those funny squiggles and little hats in the Kurdish bit.)

145

Then I cut and pasted the Kurdish version into the Word document and printed it off.

'Let's go!' said Mum, grabbing her car keys and heading for the door.

'What, now?'

'Yup – right now!'

I froze. 'Actually, I'm not sure this is such a good idea.'

'Trust me, it is,' said Mum.

'But supposing Nadima won't even talk to me?'

'That won't stop you talking to her.'

'What if her parents are angry with me?'

'Stop panicking! It'll be fine,' said Mum.

'But what if they won't even let us in the house?' I cried. 'I know – why don't we just drop it through the letter box?'

'What, and then run away?' Mum grinned.

'Yes!'

'Jaz Watson, don't be such a wimp!' She grabbed my arm and dragged me to the car.

29

❧ Sorted! ❧

Nadima's mum answered the door and, with lots of smiles, invited us in. Then she called Nadima downstairs. So of course Rasha and Sami, *and Nadima's dad*, all piled into the living room too.

I handed the note to Nadima's mum, and Nadima's dad read over her shoulder, while I stood there cringing and wanting to die of embarrassment.

Nobody spoke. It was really, really uncomfortable.

I felt more nervous than I've ever felt in front of a teacher – or even Mrs C.

I noticed that Nadima didn't try to read the note. I wasn't sure if it was because she was angry with me, or because it wasn't the way she behaved with her parents. But then they handed her the note. She read it and then they all did a lot of pulling faces and shrugging and chatting among themselves in Kurdish.

I looked anxiously at Mum.

Finally Nadima turned to me, held out the note and said, 'Is make no sense.'

'What?!' I said.

Everyone looked at everyone else.

Something must have gone horribly wrong.

Then Nadima had the (rather brilliant) idea of translating the Kurdish *back* into English on her phone. She showed me the screen.

It read:

I'm sorry Don trouble.
I did not know that it was
against the rules for the sale
of products in schools.
Please I can not be
promising not to.

I struggled to read it (obviously) so Mum read it out loud.

Nadima was right. It made *absolutely* no sense!

'What? How can that possibly be how the computer translated my note?' I cried.

Mum shrugged. 'It's a machine! That's why I'm always telling you *not* to get it to do your French homework for you!'

(Fyi, she's right. Our French teacher says Google Translate is even worse at French than 7R.)

'That is not what I wrote!' I said slowly to Nadima. I put my hand out for her phone. She handed it to me, and between us, and after a lot of typing and deleting and *retyping* and *even more deleting*, I finally managed to type what I was trying to say.

By now, Mum and Nadima's parents were sitting round the dining table drinking black coffee out of tiny little cups. Sami had clambered up onto Mum's lap, where Mum was giving him a cuddle. Rasha was shyly offering her some Turkish Delight. I groaned, remembering there must be *tons* of it in the kitchen.

Nadima showed her parents the final version of my note.

'Aaaah!' they both said, and there was a lot of smiling and laughing and nodding.

Then her mum smiled at me gently and said, 'Jaz! Is OK. Yes! You are Nadima friend.'

'You are *good* friend,' added Nadima. 'You not *bad* friend,' she added and pulled a face. 'I sorry.'

'No, *I'm* sorry,' I said.

'Ah, yes. *I'm* sorry,' repeated Nadima. She thought I was correcting her English! 'Thank you!' she added.

I gave up and just hugged her.

'See?' said Mum, as we got into the car. 'I told you it'd be fine!'

I grinned at her. Yes, it was fine. Better than fine in fact, it was *brilliant!* I pulled my feet up onto the seat and hugged my knees happily. Then I plugged Mum's phone in and we sang along to her truly *ancient* songs all the way home.

30

BFFs

The next morning was Saturday and Nad came round. Matt was going for a hair cut so he offered to drop us off at the street market.

I don't think Nad had been to the market before.

'Is wonderful!' Her eyes lit up as she looked around the brightly covered stalls.

'It's not *that* good!' I laughed.

But she just grinned and said, 'Is like at home. We have market. I love market.'

Nadima *literally* dragged me over to look at some scarves. 'Ooooh!' she breathed, picking up a dark orange one. 'Is beautiful! What is called?'

'Scarf,' I said.

'Scarf. I have same like this,' she told me. 'But is lost.'

'Oh,' I said, then couldn't think of anything more useful to say.

'That'd look lovely on you,' the woman on the stall was saying. 'Go on, try it on.'

But Nadima put it back.

'She doesn't speak much English,' I explained.

'I do speak much English!' cried Nadima, giving me a friendly shove. 'I speak lot of English!' which made me and the stallholder laugh.

Then Nad slid a midnight-blue scarf off the rack and held it up against my face.

'Is good. Blue. Is like eyes!' she declared. She showed me how to wrap it round my head the way she wore hers.

The stallholder smiled. 'She's right. It matches your eyes!'

Nadima turned to the woman. 'Is how much?'

'Eight pounds, love.'

'Eight?' Nad shrugged at me sadly. 'Is too much. Sorry. I have five.' She unwound it from my head and put it back on the stall.

There were some racks of jewellery on the back of the stall. But there was nothing for a fiver. Nadima picked up some long dangly dark blue earrings and held them up against my face. But they were for pierced ears and mine aren't pierced.

'No holes!' I said, pulling at my earlobes.

'Ahh!' she laughed. 'I make for you!?' she joked, miming.

'No way!' I cried, grabbing my ears protectively.

Then I noticed a pack of two bracelets for £8. They were twisted threads with metal hearts hanging off them. One was pink and silver, the other blue and gold. The hearts had something engraved on them in curly letters. Too curly for me to read, but I thought I could guess. 'Does that say "BFF"?' I asked the stallholder. 'I can't read it from here.'

She nodded, handing them to me.

I held them up to show Nadima. 'For us!' I said. 'Look,' and, pointing at the hearts, I explained '"BFF" – it means "Best Friends Forever"!'

Her eyes lit up and her face broke into a huge grin. 'I like!'

'Only four pounds each!' I said, holding up four fingers and pointing at her and then at me.

We bought them.

I gave Nadima first pick. She chose the blue and gold one (which was the nicest) and instantly gave it to me!

As we tied the bracelets onto each other's wrists I asked her, 'Did you have a best friend at home, in Syria?'

Her face did that tight thing it does when she's upset.

'Yes. She is called Jamal.'

I noticed she said '*is* called,' not '*was* called', so I asked, 'Is she still there?'

She frowned and looked away.

'I'm sorry,' I said, going to put my arm around her.

But she shrugged me off lightly.

'Is OK. Maybe she OK. I hope she OK. I hope.'

'What's she like, Jamal?'

She smiled warmly as she remembered her. 'She funny. She kind. She clever. Jamal like you!' she said.

31
Crown Jewels

When I got into class on Monday, Nadima was showing off her bracelet to Chloe and Elly.

'That's *sooo* pretty,' said Elly.

'I've got one too,' I said, leaning over Nadima and showing them the one on my wrist. 'They're a pair.'

So then Elly turned to Chloe. 'Shall we get some?'

'Only if I get the pink and silver one,' said Chloe.

'OMG, Chloe, you're so pink!' I laughed, and the others joined in.

At which point Kara arrived, with Lily. So of course she instantly demanded to know what we were laughing at.

When Elly explained, Kara literally *grabbed* Nadima's wrist. 'Ooooh, let's see!'

'Is pretty, yes?' Nadima smiled.

'Yes, it's lovely. Look, Lily – it's got "Best Friends Forever" on the heart,' said Kara.

My stomach suddenly went all cold. Why hadn't I thought about how Lily would feel about me and Nad having BFF bracelets? I would have been gutted if she and Kara had got a pair. Why hadn't I thought about her?

I watched her face anxiously. She leaned over to look closely at my bracelet. I was literally holding my breath. But all she said was, 'I love the little heart!'

I can't tell you how relieved I was, but then Elly said, 'We're getting some,' gesturing to herself and Chloe.

So of course Kara turned to Lily and said, 'Let's get some too!'

Lily nodded eagerly and said, 'OK!'

My stomach flipped and I felt sick.

So was that it? Lil and I weren't best friends any more? She was now, officially, *best friends* with Kara – *forever*. My throat was closing up and any minute I was going to have to rush off to the loo – either that or burst into tears in front of the whole of 7R.

But then Lil did something typically lovely and, well, typically Lily.

She smiled at me and said, 'Then we can all be BFFs together!' And the knots in my stomach melted like chocolate in a chocolate fountain.

So Monday morning got off to *fabulous* start. And then it got even better, because straight after registration Mrs W reminded us that next week was Charity Challenge Week.

'Everyone's got to come up with their best fundraising ideas,' she told us. 'And there are *prizes* for the people who raise the most money!'

Ryan and Liam punched the air with a 'Yes!' and everyone else instantly started chatting excitedly about what they could do.

LOL! I thought. There was no way anyone else was going to get a look in. I was going to *ace* the Charity Challenge by getting more money than anyone else had *ever* raised in the *entire* history of the school *ever*!

I was still in a good mood when we all trooped into drama (which was a first for me). Mrs P told us all to just pick up where we'd left off working up our box stories. Everyone seemed to know exactly what they were doing – except Nadima and me. We hadn't even come up with an idea.

Nadima took out her drama book and a pen. 'We make story, yes?' she said.

Yeah, right, like it's that simple, I thought. Fyi, I'm absolutely rubbish at making up stories. I literally don't know how to do it.

I put up my hand, so Mrs P twirled over, her kaftan billowing behind her.

'It's impossible,' I told her. 'Nadima simply doesn't have enough English to make up a story.'

'What happened to the idea you were working on last week?' she said, gathering up the flowing folds of her kaftan and sitting on the floor.

I *literally* winced when I realised she meant my Turkish Delight scheme. 'Um, well, it didn't work out,' I said truthfully.

'Well, then you'll just have to make up another one,' announced Mrs P.

'But I don't even know where to start!' I wailed.

Nadima raised her eyebrows at me, and the rest of the class looked over – hoping for some *real* drama, no doubt.

'Oh, well, I can help you with that!' declared Mrs P. 'We can easily find a good starting point for a story. What sort of things do you both like? Hmmm?'

Why am I meant to know the sort of things Nadima likes?

I know loads of stuff about Lily – her favourite colour (turquoise), lucky number (7), choice of pizza (ham and pineapple). I know which bands, and movies and even which books she likes. I know she loves ice-skating and has always wanted a Palomino pony called Star. But how was I supposed to know what Nadima liked?

And then, like the genius I am, I remembered our first emoji conversation.

'Hang on!' I cried, grabbing my phone and quickly trawling through my texts. 'I can tell you *exactly* what we both like!' I told Mrs P. 'Music and dancing and going to the movies . . . and popcorn and burgers and chips . . . and pizza and cake and ice cream . . . and chocolate,' I said. Then I remembered our BFF bracelets and added, 'And jewellery.'

'Brilliant! Brilliant!' gushed Mrs P. 'So you both like *jewellery*, and the theme is "A Box", so you could have . . . ?' She looked at me expectantly.

'Er . . . a jewellery box?' I said.

'Yes! Brilliant! Maybe you could start with some jewels, or some *treasure*! How about if some

159

priceless jewels go missing – stolen maybe?' she said excitedly.

'What, like stealing the Crown Jewels?' I asked sarcastically.

Ignoring the sarcasm, Mrs P said, 'Well, yes, why not? Yes, actually, brilliant, brilliant! That's a wonderful idea. Make up a story about stealing the Crown Jewels!'

And with that she hitched up her kaftan, got up off the floor and went off.

What a totally rubbish idea, I thought. But it was better than nothing, so I sighed heavily, got out my phone and googled 'crwon jewls' and showed the picture to Nadima.

'Aha! Yes! Crown Jewels. Royal Family. Queen Elizabeth. Buckingham Palace!' she said with a huge grin.

I burst out laughing. It was crazy the words she knew. But I guess those are words lots of tourists know. Not that she's a tourist of course.

'We have to make up a story about someone trying to steal the Crown Jewels,' I said.

'I not understand,' she said. So I typed 'steal' into my phone and showed her the Kurdish word.

She pretended to gasp and joked, 'We *steal* Crown Jewels? Jaz! NO!'

We both burst out laughing. That was as far as we got, because Mrs P was asking some of the groups to show everyone what they'd done so far.

Obviously she started with her favourite pupil. So we all had to watch Kara and Lily *melodramatically* finding a baby in the snow. Kara was the star of course, the one actually finding the baby. Lily was doing snowy sound effects in the background.

'Whoosh, whoooo, whooosh,' she went.

Kara pretended she was clutching a baby and battling against the storm, until Lily suddenly jumped out and started growling like a bear or a Yeti or something.

Kara acted all terrified, cradling the baby and cowering. But then she started singing and 'tamed' the Yeti (or the bear or whatever). So Lily lay down on the floor and then, thankfully, it ended.

'That's as far as we've got,' Kara babbled, acting all modest.

'Marvellous, marvellous!' trilled Mrs P, clapping like crazy.

7R cringed on her behalf.

Then she picked on Liam and Ryan. They got up and acted out some action-packed scenes from *Star Wars* or something. They did a lot of rushing around and shouting mad stuff at each other like, 'Take that!' and, 'Aaaaargh!' and, 'KABOOM!' and, 'BSHHHHH!' It was completely baffling, but it ended in a massive lightsabre fight (with full sound effects) and both of them died. Their death throes were awesome, btw. Everyone applauded wildly. So they both sprang up and bowed theatrically.

Mrs P was speechless.

Kara was dead jealous. 'What's any of that got to do with a box?' she demanded.

LOL.

Fortunately the bell went before Mrs P could pick on anyone else.

So everyone grabbed their bags and made a bid for freedom.

'Well done, 7R,' trilled Mrs P. 'And I'm really looking forward to seeing your story, Jaz!' she shouted after us, as Nadima and I escaped down the corridor.

Honestly, how are Nadima and I meant to work out how to make up a story about stealing the Crown Jewels? It'd be easier to *literally* steal the Crown Jewels.

Don't you just HATE it when teachers set you work that's actually *impossible* to do – so you're absolutely destined to fail – and in front of the whole class? Do they even stop to think before they dream up these stupid projects?

Apparently not.

If I thought the drama project was stupid, I was gobsmacked at the homework our history teacher set us.

It was OFF THE STUPID SCALE ENTIRELY.

32
Families

We were doing the Tudors in history. Which, as far as I could make out, is mostly just learning the list of wives Henry VIII either divorced or beheaded before nipping off to rob all the monasteries. (What a charmer.)

So for some stupid reason our history teacher, Mrs B, told us all to do our own family trees for homework. This instantly set Kara off on a full-blown melodrama at lunchtime. We'd only just done eating when she kicked off. With a huge amount of hair flicking she announced, 'I'm not doing it. I'm not putting my lousy stepdad and his horrible kids onto a "family tree" and making it look like we're all one big happy family!' she fumed.

'Can't you just leave them off?' suggested Chloe.

'Even if I do – where am I supposed to put *my* dad?'

164

'Aren't you supposed to put him next to your mum?' said Elly.

'I can't do that!' Kara wailed. 'It'll look like they're still married – and they're not, are they?'

'Why don't you just add a little note explaining they're divorced?' asked Lily.

Kara whipped round furiously. *'Just add a little note?* What, because *a little note* can explain what it means when your parents get divorced?!'

'I didn't mean that!' Lily went bright red. 'All I meant was there must be a way of putting a divorce on a family tree. Why don't you ask other people what they're going to put? Like Jaz! Her parents are divorced too!'

'Lily!' I cried, furiously.

'Are they?' asked Chloe.

'I didn't know that,' said Elly.

'Thanks, Lil!' I said. 'Why not tell everybody?'

'What's the problem? It's not a secret,' she snapped.

'That doesn't mean to say I want everyone gossiping about it!'

'You're just both making a huge fuss about this!' she announced.

'How would you know? We don't all have your perfect family!' I snapped back.

165

Lily looked like I'd slapped her. So then Kara put her arm around her and had a go at me! 'Don't be so mean, Jaz!'

'You started it!' I cried.

Kara didn't reply. She was too busy comforting Lily.

Honestly. I don't know why I'm trying to be nice to Kara. She *always* ends up doing something like that. She *always* manages to get between me and Lily.

I walked off.

How did that happen anyway? How did I end up in the wrong when it was Kara who started being mean to Lily in the first place?

Obviously Kara didn't give me a chance to talk to Lily for the rest of the day, so I started to text her from the school bus.

Lil
I'm really sorry about what I said about your family. I didn't mean it.
I was just upset because

But then I realised I couldn't put that last bit because the reason I was upset was that Lily had told everyone about my dad. So if I went on about that then it would just make it worse.

So I deleted the last bit and hit send.

The more I thought about doing the family-tree homework, the more it started to bug me. I've always been fine, really, with not having a dad. I don't even remember him – I was so little when he left. But there are some things that are private, aren't there? I really *didn't* want to put him on it – and I could *absolutely* see why Kara wanted to leave her stepdad off hers. I wondered if I should ask Mum about it, but I was worried it might upset her – she never talks about my dad.

Then I started feeling angry. What makes my history teacher think she has the right to know stuff about me, and my family? How would she like it if I asked her if she was divorced, or if her ex-husband had got married again? We don't know anything about our teachers' private lives – so how come they get to poke their noses into ours?

33

'D' Means 'Died'

I'd promised to help Nadima with her family tree, so on Thursday evening I went round to her house after I'd made supper. (Chicken in barbecue sauce – with chips *and* salad. Impressive or what!) Nadima's mum was carrying Sami upstairs.

He flung his arms out at me. 'Jaz! Jaz!' he demanded.

Nadima's mum shot me a questioning look. 'Is OK?' she asked.

I grinned and took Sami and plonked him on my hip.

'Is bathtime,' said Nad, so we went up to the bathroom.

The sides of the bath, and the tiled wall above it, were covered with those coloured foam letters – all spelling out the English word for things like 'tap', 'soap', 'sink' and 'toilet'.

Nadima ran a bath and put Sami in it. Then I

made soapy bubbles and let him pop them. Every time his little finger burst a bubble I went, 'POP!' and he'd collapse into a huge belly laugh.

'Sami, say, "Pop!"' I said. He looked at Nadima and then back at me and then he screwed up his podgy little mouth, and went, 'Pop!' It was *sooo* cute! Then, after we'd dried him, we bundled him into a nappy and his night onesie. It was only the sweetest thing *ever*, with floppy-eared baby bunny rabbits all over it.

'Bunnies!' I said to Sami, pointing at them.

'No, Jaz, is rabbits!' Nadima frowned.

Seriously!? Her English is getting so good she's even correcting me now!

After Sami was in bed, Nad and I started on our homework. We sat round the table in the living room while Nadima's mum put Rasha to bed. I thought if I did my family tree first, then Nad could copy it.

I started with my mum. 'Kate Watson. My mum.' I said, writing her name down in the middle of the paper. I added her date of birth next to it. 'Her birthday,' I said.

Nadima nodded.

Then I put a little "m" next to Mum's name and

wrote "Tom Watson". My dad. I didn't put his date of birth – I didn't know when it was. 'The "m" means they're married,' I explained.

'Yes. Married.' Nadima nodded. 'Kate Watson married Tom Watson,' she said, pointing to the words to show she understood.

'Yes. No! Wait! Hang on a minute!' I said. I realised I'd made a mistake. I crossed out 'Watson' after 'Kate' and wrote 'Cooper' instead. 'My mum was called "Cooper",' I explained. 'Before she married my dad.'

Then I drew a line down from the 'm' and another line across the bottom of that line and wrote my brother's names on it, and then mine.

'See? This means we are their children,' I explained.

'Yes, OK.' Then she pointed at my dad's name. '*Tom Watson* – he is your dad?' she asked slowly.

'Yes,' I replied.

She looked at me expectantly. 'He not here?' she asked gently.

'No,' I said. 'He left us. He went away.'

'Oh,' she said, and then gave a huge sigh of relief. 'I think maybe he dead.'

'No!' I cried. 'They're divorced. Not married any more.'

170

'Is sad,' said Nadima, and her dark eyes filled with sympathy.

'It was ages ago,' I shrugged. 'We never see him.'

Her face fell and she said, 'Oh, Jaz. Is more sad,' and she put her arm round me.

It's a funny thing, but it hadn't really hit me before. It *was* sad, I realised. He left just after I was born and we haven't seen him since. He can't even be bothered to send us a Christmas card or remember our birthdays. He doesn't even know what I look like. We could have all *died* for all he cares. I suddenly wished I hadn't put him on my family tree. Partly because I don't actually want to have to talk about him, but mostly because he doesn't deserve to be there. He's not part of my family, is he?

I decided that when I got home I would rip the page out of my book and do the family tree all over again – and leave him off entirely.

I quickly drew in the lines above my mum and added my granny and grampa's names. I had absolutely no idea what their dates of birth were – I'd have to ask Mum. But I did know when Grampa died. It was two years ago. So I wrote 'd' and added the year.

Nadima pointed at the 'd'. 'What is mean?' she asked.

'"D" for died. Dead,' I explained.

'Oh,' she said quietly.

I closed my book and we did Nadima's family tree. She started off fine. She quickly wrote in her parents' names, and then added Sami, Rasha and herself. Then she drew lines from both her parents and started adding the names of her uncles and aunties.

'My Uncle Tarek. Uncle Nizar. Aunt Amena. Here my Aunt Zada and my Uncle Sayid. And here my Uncle Karam and my Aunt Ranim.'

'You've got a lot of uncles and aunties!' I joked.

'Yes. Also lots of children!' she said.

'Children! You have children?' I teased, deliberately misunderstanding her.

'NO! Aunt and uncle children,' she laughed.

'Cousins,' I said.

'*Cousins*,' she repeated, and then she added all her cousins' names.

'You have a HUGE family!' I said. 'Have you got any photos of them?'

She paused, just for a beat, and then she said, 'Yes,' and opened up their laptop.

With such a big family I was expecting *hundreds* of pictures. But there weren't. There were only a few. She clicked through them quickly – some kids playing football, a couple of women in a cafe cuddling toddlers on their laps, a pile of children all crammed together on a sofa, laughing at something, her mum and dad in a garden with a baby.

I pointed at the baby. 'Sami?' I asked.

'Yes. At my home.'

The last photo was of lots of people having a meal together. Everyone was laughing and smiling.

'This is Eid,' she said. 'Is big party.'

'Is big family!' I joked, and she smiled.

I pointed at a little girl who looked a bit like Nadima. 'Is that you, when you were little?'

'No. Is Ishtar. Cousin. And this her baby sister Amira. No photo of little me.'

'What? No photos of you as a baby or anything?'

'No. We lose photos. These on phone when we come here.'

'Nadima! That's really sad!' I said.

She shrugged, turned away and went back to doing her family tree.

Very slowly and carefully, and very neatly, she

started putting little 'd's against the names of some of her aunts and uncles.

'Nadima, the "d" means "dead",' I reminded her awkwardly. 'Is that right? Are these people . . . dead?'

She nodded. 'Yes. Is right.'

Then something splashed onto the paper, smudging the ink. She was crying – but totally silently. Tears streamed down her face, but she kept on writing.

'Nadima, stop! You don't have to do this,' I said, putting my arm around her.

But she shrugged me off and started adding in more little 'd's – this time next to some of her cousins' names. By now she was sobbing. A horrible, gasping sort of sob.

'Nadima! Stop! Please stop!' I begged, and I tried to take the pen off her. But she snatched it away and carried on writing – but she couldn't see for crying. It was like a floodgate had opened. She was shaking and sobbing and I couldn't do anything to stop her.

I ran upstairs two at a time to get her mum. She was curled around Rasha on the bottom bunk, singing to her softly. They jumped as I burst into the room. I grabbed her arm and pulled at her.

'Come, please come!' I said urgently. They both leaped up, panic-stricken. Rasha looked terrified.

'It's Nadima. She's crying!' I said.

I tried to signal to Rasha to stay in bed, but she clung on to her mother's hand and they raced downstairs.

Nadima was slumped over her homework with her head on her arms, sobbing and gasping. Rasha's eyes were huge with fear and she started crying too. Gently, Nadima's mum pulled Nadima into a hug and spoke to her in Kurdish. Nadima sobbed some words back. Her mum looked at the homework and at the photo still open on the laptop, then slowly, as if the reality of what she was seeing was sinking in, her whole face crumpled in agony. Clutching Nadima and Rasha to her, she started sobbing too . . . sobbing and rocking, sobbing and rocking.

It was horrible. I didn't know what to do. There didn't seem to be anything I *could* do. I went upstairs to make sure Sami was all right. I was worried they might have woken him. But he was fast asleep, with a little fluffy blue teddy under one arm, breathing softly through his little mouth. Mum always says that when we were little kids we could sleep anywhere – and through any amount of noise. 'Bombproof,' she used to joke.

But little kids aren't bombproof.

People aren't bombproof.

Nadima's aunts and uncles and cousins were not bombproof.

I left Sami sleeping safe and sound and went back downstairs.

I stood in the doorway, watching Nadima's family. Her mum had wrapped both girls tightly in her arms. She was still sobbing and rocking her big bundle of sadness.

I was just in the way, so I let myself out the front door. I closed it very quietly so I didn't disturb them, but I listened to make sure it shut properly, with them safe inside. Then I walked home.

I've seen lots of people cry. And not just little kids. I've seen Lily cry, and some of my other friends, and I've seen all of The Brothers cry. I've even seen grown-ups cry – not very often, but I have. Mum cried at Grampa's funeral.

But I'd never seen anyone cry like that. I'd never seen anyone hurting so much.

34
Isolation

The next morning, Friday, I stormed into school and barged into the staffroom. I didn't even bother to knock. I just went straight up to Mrs B, our history teacher, and started yelling at her.

The entire staffroom froze.

'Have you any idea how stupid that family-tree homework was?' I shouted. 'I went round to Nadima's to help her, and it turns out that loads of her family died back in Syria. *Loads of them*. Her family tree is covered with little "d"s. "D" for "*dead*",' I reminded her. 'You upset Nadima and her whole family! They were *sobbing*, literally sobbing!'

By now Mrs B had gone white and the whole staffroom had gone dead silent.

'Did you even stop to think before you set it?' I went on. 'Or did you think, "Oh, I know, I've got a refugee in my class from Syria, so I'll just get her to make a chart of her entire family, including when they were born – *and when they died*."

Mrs B's hand flew to her mouth. She looked stunned. Out of the corner of my eye I could see Mrs C bearing down on me – but I hadn't finished yet.

'What right do you have to go poking into our lives? Asking us all about our family secrets. And making people remember things, horrible, dreadful things. Who do you think you are?' By now Mrs B looked like she was going to cry.

'JAZ WATSON! That is enough!' bawled Mrs C. 'My office. Now.'

Mrs C virtually dragged me into her office and slammed the door. As usual she sat down and left me standing in front of her desk. But I didn't care. I was standing up for Nadima.

'How dare you burst into the staffroom and start yelling at a member of my staff like that?' she demanded.

'Because she –'

She put her hand up to stop me. 'It is completely unacceptable and I will not tolerate it.'

'But Mrs B –'

'Do *not* interrupt me.'

178

How unfair was that? She wasn't even giving me a chance to explain.

'I would class your outburst as "aggressive behaviour" towards a teacher and, you might be interested to know, that would give me the right to formally exclude you from school.'

I gasped. *Exclude me?*

'Do you understand me?' she snapped.

'Yes, but can I just explain . . . ?'

'No, you may not.'

'But that's not fair!' I yelled.

Mrs C sat there icily calm and raised one eyebrow in warning. 'Don't raise your voice to me, young lady. I have heard more than enough from you this morning. You will go to the isolation room and stay there until break. I am going to call your mother, and then all three of us will discuss your behaviour. Then I'll decide what to do next.'

I strode out of her office and into the isolation room, just down the corridor. I sat there with my arms folded, seething. She could exclude me if she wanted to. I didn't care! What was more important to me was sticking up for Nadima and her family. And what's more, I knew Mum would back me up.

Oh, how wrong could I be?

35

Furious

Mum sat opposite Mrs C, in her office, tight-lipped and worried.

For once I got to sit down too. But I had to sit there *in silence* while Mrs C gave Mum a blow-by-blow account of what had happened in the staffroom. So of course Mum only got her side of the story. How I'd 'burst' in and started 'bawling' at the history teacher 'at the top of my voice' and in 'an entirely inappropriate way' and 'completely unprovoked'!

It was totally unfair. Mrs C made it sound like it was *all my fault*! Like her precious teacher hadn't done anything wrong at all! But when I tried to explain, Mum shut me up with a look.

I slumped back angrily in my seat, with my arms folded.

Then Mrs C went on about how 'aggressive and

threatening' I'd been, and how 'shaken and upset' the teacher was afterwards. Honestly, she made it sound like I'd actually attacked her! Finally, Mrs C stopped and Mum turned to me.

'Jaz, I'm shocked and . . . and . . .' she struggled to find the right word, '. . . *appalled* by your behaviour!' she said.

'But I was standing up for Nadima and her family!' I protested. 'I was only telling her what her stupid homework had done to them!'

'Bawling at your teacher in the staffroom was not the way to do it,' snapped Mum.

'So, what, we're not allowed to tell a teacher their *stupid* homework was *stupid* and thoughtless and cruel and had Nadima's family in tears?' I argued hotly.

'Not if you do it by blasting into the staffroom and losing your temper,' said Mum.

Then Mrs C pitched in. 'I didn't put you in isolation for telling a teacher the homework was insensitive, Jaz. I isolated you because of your aggressive behaviour towards her.'

'I wasn't aggressive!' I yelled.

'Well, you're being aggressive now!' snapped Mum. 'Just calm down.'

Furiously, I threw myself back in my chair.

Mrs C turned to Mum. 'Mrs Watson, by rights I could exclude Jaz from school, but I'd prefer not to.'

'I'd prefer you didn't too,' said Mum. She'd gone white.

'I'm going to put her back into isolation until lunchtime,' Mrs C carried on. 'I'd rather leave you to deal with her than have to exclude her.'

'Thank you,' said Mum. 'And obviously Jaz will apologise to the teacher concerned.'

'What?!' I gasped.

I could not believe what I was hearing! Mrs C stood up. 'Thanks very much for coming straight in, Mrs Watson. It's very reassuring when we know we have the support of the parents.'

Mum nodded, then she turned to me. 'We'll talk about this later, Jaz,' she said. and left the room without even saying goodbye. I'd never seen her so angry.

I spent the next two lessons banged up in isolation doing maths. The time dragged and dragged. I was desperate for the day to end. I knew I was going home to a major roasting – and I just wanted to get it over and done with.

*

As soon as the bell went for lunch I went to find Nadima, to make sure she was all right. I saw her heading over to the canteen with the others.

'Nadima!' I called and she came rushing over.

'Jaz! Is OK?' she asked anxiously.

'Yes! Everything's fine,' I lied. I didn't want to get sidetracked into talking about me. 'Are *you* all right?' I asked her. 'And your mum, and Rasha? Are you all OK? After last night, I mean.'

The anxious look slid off her face and she smiled at me. 'Yes. Thank you, Jaz. Yes. We OK.'

'I was worried. You were all so upset.'

She shrugged. 'Is sad. Is very sad. We cry. Lots.'

I nodded and I went to put my arm round her. But she slipped her arm through mine instead.

'Today is new day,' she said. 'Is lunch! I am hungry. Come on!' and she pulled me towards the canteen.

The others had kept a couple of spaces for us. As soon as I sat down they practically mobbed me. They all knew where'd I'd been, of course. But they didn't know why. No one in our class had ever been in isolation before, and the rumour factory had been working overtime.

'Somebody said you'd stormed into the staffroom

and punched a teacher!' gasped Kara, her eyes shining.

'Was it Mr Y?' asked Chloe.

'I bet it was!' cried Elly.

'I didn't hit anyone!' I said.

'Well, what happened then?' asked Lily. 'Must've been something dead serious.'

'Are you getting expelled?' asked Chloe breathlessly.

'No, course not!' I said heatedly. And then – and I'm *not kidding* – she actually looked disappointed!

Tactless or what?!

Honestly, they were all behaving like a pack of vultures.

So I started to tell them *exactly* what I'd said to Mrs B. As soon as I got to the bit where I reminded her that Nadima came from Syria, Lily cut in.

'Syria?' she said, and turning to Nadima she added, 'You come from Syria?'

Nadima shot me a quick look and then she nodded at Lily. 'Yes. I am from Syria.'

Everyone went quiet and stared at Nadima. Nobody knew what to say. Even Elly and Chloe had heard about what was happening in Syria. And for once Kara didn't go all melodramatic.

Nadima's eyes flicked round the girls' faces, one after another. I think she was scared about how they were going to react. I wished I hadn't mentioned Syria at all. So I said, 'I don't think Nadima wants to talk about Syria. It's very bad over there.'

Lily leaned across the table and took hold of Nadima's hand. 'I've seen it on the news,' she said. 'It looks terrible.'

'Yes. Is very bad,' Nadima said quietly.

'You don't have to talk about it, if you don't want to,' said Lily.

Nadima nodded tightly and managed a small smile.

36

Stupid!

I lay on my bed absolutely *dreading* the moment when Mum came home. When I heard her key in the lock I froze. She was going to be OFF THE SCALE angry. She yelled up at me to come downstairs before she'd even shut the front door. Then she went into the living room and we sat at either end of the sofa.

'I'm not angry, Jaz,' she started.

Yes, you are! I thought.

She carried on, 'You had a good point. A very good point about the homework . . .'

'So why didn't you stick up for me?' I demanded.

'Because you blew it by going in all guns blazing! So now the focus isn't on the insensitivity of the homework –'

'The *stupid* insensitivity of the homework,' I cut in.

186

'*Now* the focus is on you yelling at your teacher! Now *that* was stupid. And wrong!'

'I was angry,' I muttered.

'I know, but getting angry isn't the way to deal with things. And *when* you're angry isn't the *time* to deal with things!'

I sat with my arms folded and didn't reply.

She sighed. 'I'm worried about you, Jaz. You keep getting yourself into trouble.'

'I don't "*get myself*" into trouble!' I protested.

'Yes, you do! You keep challenging the rules all the time.'

'Only the stupid ones. Anyway, half the time I don't even know they're rules!'

'Look, I know school can be a bit of a struggle, and maybe doing the family tree was tricky for you because of your –'

'THIS IS NOT ABOUT MY DYSLEXIA!' I yelled. She reeled back. 'And I am *not* struggling in school! I just won a maths medal – which is more than the boys have ever done!' I reminded her.

'I'm trying to help you, Jaz. If you carry on like this you're going to get yourself excluded.'

I couldn't believe I'd heard right.

'I'm not going to "*get myself*" excluded,' I raged, 'Kids don't "*get themselves*" excluded! It's teachers who exclude kids! And Mrs C – who, in case you didn't notice, didn't even give me a chance to defend myself!'

I got up and stormed out.

'Jaz! JAZ!' called Mum. 'We haven't finished talking!'

'Yes, we have!' I bawled, stomping up to my room.

I threw myself onto my bed, raging hot inside.

Texts pinged into my phone all evening. Everyone was making sure I was OK. At least my friends cared about me – even if my mum didn't.

I barely spoke at supper. Mum carried on as if everything was all right, chatting away to the boys and trying to pull me into the conversation. But I ignored her.

I spent the evening in my room, texting. I thought Mum would come up. She didn't. So I slipped into bed without even going down to say goodnight. And then I lay there wide awake – for ages. My brain kept churning over everything that had happened. Eventually I heard her go to bed, but she didn't even tap on my door. So I slid out of bed and went to her room. I wasn't going in to say sorry. I just wanted to put her right on something.

'I just want to explain about the family-tree homework,' I said.

'OK,' she said, sitting up and patting the space on the bed next to her.

I sat next to her with my legs crossed. 'I really didn't have a problem *doing* it. I'm good at charts. But I did have a problem with *having* to do it. I just don't think the teachers should have the right to make us tell them stuff about us – personal stuff – that we might not want them to know. And it wasn't only Nadima's family it upset. Kara was upset too. She didn't want to have to put her stepdad onto her family tree, or his kids. Or leave her real dad off just because she didn't know how to show that her mum and dad are divorced.'

Mum was quiet for a moment, and then she asked, 'Did you put your dad on your family tree?'

Which sort of threw me for a second. 'Yes,' I said. 'But I'm going to do it again without him.'

'Oh, great!' She laughed. 'So your teacher will think I've had four kids without even being married! That'll get them talking in the staffroom!'

189

'That's *exactly* my point!' I cried. 'It's none of their business!'

Then she went all serious. 'You don't have to put him on if you don't want to.'

'I'm not going to. Why should I? He's *not* part of our family – and anyway, I can't even remember him.'

She went over to the wardrobe and got out the box of family photos from the very back, from behind the Christmas decorations, and dumped it on the bed. Then she dug out a picture, from right at the bottom, and handed it to me.

'That's your dad,' she said.

'I didn't know you had a photo of him. Why didn't you show me it before?'

She shrugged. 'You never asked.'

She was right. I hadn't asked before. I knew I hadn't. I'd never been interested before. It was only now. Because of the stupid family-tree homework, I suppose.

I took the photo from her. 'He looks like Matt!'

'Yes, doesn't he?' She smiled. 'You take more after me. Bad luck!' she joked.

Looking at the photo, the man smiling out at me seemed a nice enough bloke. It's just that he

190

wasn't. Well, he couldn't be, could he? Not if he'd just gone off and left us.

Mum was flicking through the rest of the photos. 'Here's one of my favourites,' she said, 'Matt's first birthday.' She handed me a picture of a baby, sitting in a highchair with his face *completely* plastered with chocolate.

'How can you tell who it is under all that chocolate?' I laughed.

'Easy!' she said. 'After I'd discovered just how much mess one small baby could make with just a handful of milk-chocolate buttons, I always bought white-chocolate ones after that!'

I wondered why she'd kept a photo of my dad – even if it was buried right at the bottom of a box.

'Do you miss him? My dad, I mean.'

She came and sat next to me on the bed. 'No, I don't miss him. Although I do think I miss having a husband,' she said thoughtfully. 'It has been a bit tough, dragging you lot up on my own. I just don't miss that one!'

That was exactly it. I didn't miss *my* dad – but I did miss having *a* dad.

And I know it's stupid, but I suddenly felt jealous

of everyone who does have a dad. Especially Lily. She's got a great dad. And look at Kara – she's got two! Even if that does make her life a bit messy. At least her real dad stuck around after her parents got divorced. And then there's Nadima. I know I shouldn't feel jealous of Nadima, not after everything she's been through, but I was. Her dad seemed really nice when I met him, and sort of . . . oh, I dunno, steady and reliable and . . . well, just there.

Then I looked at Mum flicking through the family photos and I thought, Who needs a dad when you've got a great mum like mine?!

I put my arms round her and hugged her. 'Love you, Mum.'

'Love you more,' she said with a smile, hugging me back.

37
Charity Challenge Week

First thing on Monday morning I headed to the staffroom. I was *soooo* not looking forward to this. There's nothing worse than a gloating teacher, is there?

Apparently there is.

It's a whole room full gloating teachers.

(Groan.)

But anyhow I did it. I apologised. And I somehow even managed to make it sound like I really meant it. (I didn't, *obviously*.)

When I got finally into class, Nadima was the centre of attention. It turns out that Mrs C had emailed her parents to say how sorry she was that the history homework had upset them so much.

Huh! I thought. She should have said sorry the stupid homework had been set *at all*. But it was better than nothing, I supposed.

Just then our form teacher arrived, so we all slid into our seats. I suddenly had this *brilliant* image of our history teacher being made to stand in front of Mrs C's desk while Mrs C told her off!

'D'you think Mrs B got a roasting?' I whispered to Lily.

She grinned. 'Yup!'

'Serves her right!'

'Again, yup!'

Which made me smile.

But not as much as what Mrs W said next.

'Right, 7R. Charity Challenge Week is upon us! So that means no lessons this morning!'

Cue cheers!

Charity Challenge? Yes! I thought. This was my time to shine!

'So I hope you've all come armed with lots of brilliant fundraising ideas! Everybody will be divided into teams of six,' said Mrs W.

Everyone instantly started calling out and gesturing, until Mrs W said, 'Calm down – I've already sorted you into teams.'

Cue furious howls of indignation from the *entire* class.

'That's not fair!'

'Why can't we choose our own teams?'

'Because Charity Challenge Week is important. It's about being entrepreneurs and coming up with serious business ideas that are going to make as much money as possible for charity. It's not about larking around with your mates,' announced Mrs W pompously.

Everyone in the class slumped back miserably and looked bored to death.

'Oh, come on! Cheer up!' said Mrs W. 'There are prizes for the team that raises the most money!'

At which point everyone sat forward again, eyes glinting greedily.

'Every member of the winning team will win a book token,' announced Mrs W.

A *book token*?! I thought. Seriously? Why would I want a book token? I'd rather have cash! And I'm pretty sure the rest of 7R felt the same way too – judging by the way they all groaned and slumped back again.

LOL!

Then Mrs W added eagerly, '*And* they get to choose the local charity which will receive all the money raised by the whole school!' Funnily enough, even that awesome honour didn't get 7R leaping out of their seats with enthusiasm.

Nadima and I got put in a team with Liam and Ryan and Lily and . . . Kara.

Oh, how absolutely brilliant.

I didn't mind having Liam and Ryan – they're always good for a laugh and I figured they'd pretty much do as I told them to. Obviously I was pleased Nadima and Lily and me were together. But I just knew Kara was going to be a massive pain in the bum. And guess what? I was 100 per cent right.

'Your first task is to choose your fundraising project,' Mrs W was saying, 'so everybody move round so you can sit in your groups. You've got until break. If anyone is stuck I have some ideas here,' she finished, waving a tatty old folder around.

'We have to do something to make money,' I explained to Nadima. She nodded.

'Like washing cars,' said Ryan.

'Actually, that's not a bad idea,' said Liam.

'I am *not* washing cars!' announced Kara.

'No,' said Nadima with a dead straight face. 'Is bad idea. Break nails.'

I snorted out loud.

'Right,' said Kara, ignoring me and taking

196

charge. She got out her planner, opened it at the back and sat tapping her pen on the page. 'Ideas?' she demanded.

'How about a cake sale?' said Lily.

'Soak the teacher?' suggested Ryan.

'Battle of the Bands!' cried Liam.

Cue him and Ryan leaping up on their chairs and playing imaginary guitars – with full sound effects of course.

'Ryan and Liam, GET DOWN!' yelled Mrs W.

'There isn't enough time!' I laughed, as the boys sat back down. Fyi, each year group had been given a two-hour slot in the hall. Ours was on Thursday afternoon. 'And anyhow, your guitars are out of tune!'

It was time to roll out my brilliant ideas.

'How about "Dress Like a Zombie Day"? Everyone will want to do it and, since there are fifteen hundred kids in the school, if we charge £1 a head we'll make £1,500!'

Ryan and Liam were well up for it, and I could see Lily thought it was a good idea, but Kara pulled a face. 'I can't see any of the girls wanting to do that,' she said.

Btw, she was wrong, but it didn't matter. I had

lots more ideas. 'OK. How about a raffle for something mega like, say, a PlayStation?'

'Where are we going to get a PlayStation from!' scoffed Kara.

'We'll get a local shop to donate one. They'll do it for the publicity!' I explained. She rolled her eyes, so I gave up on that. 'Or how about the Ultimate Swap Shop. Get everyone to bring in their old clothes and stuff, and sell stuff for £1. Even if only half the school buys something, we'd still make £750!'

'I'm *not* running a second-hand clothes stall! That's a rubbish idea!' announced Kara.

'No, it's not! Actually I'm going to set up a website doing just that!'

'Yeah? Well, good luck with *that*!' she said sarcastically.

If Lily hadn't been there, I would have given Kara a right mouthful.

It was obvious she wasn't going to agree to anything *she* didn't want to do. She suggested: a fashion show, a talent show (what a surprise) and a nail bar. A nail bar?! Fortunately the boys crushed all those ideas, so I didn't have to.

'Head-shave?' cried Ryan. 'Sponsored head-shave!'

'Yes!' whooped Liam.

'Brilliant idea!' I said. (But only because I'd love to see Kara bald.)

'You're not taking this seriously,' she complained.

'Sweets?' suggested Nadima suddenly. 'Make sweets?'

We all stared at her, gobsmacked that she'd:

a) been able to follow the conversation and
b) come up with an idea.

She shrugged. 'Everyone like sweets!'

'That,' I said, remembering what her parents did for a living, 'is not a bad idea.'

Even Kara was up for it. 'I make the *best* Rocky Road!' she announced *modestly*.

'My nan makes Peppermint Creams,' said Ryan. 'She'll make a ton if I ask her.'

'We used to make that Fridge-Fudge, Jaz!' said Lily. 'D'you remember?'

Before I could answer, Kara butted in and pulled a 'sad face'. 'But I need you to make Rocky Road with me.'

Lily looked torn.

But then Nadima said, 'Is OK. Jaz with me. We make Turkish Delight.'

'But you tried selling that before and nobody wanted to buy it!' objected Kara.

She was right, but I didn't want to crush Nadima. My dream of breaking the school record for fundraising crumbled like a chocolate flake.

Then Nadima grinned and announced, 'Ah, but this time, we make . . . with chocolate!'

'*Chocolate* Turkish Delight?' repeated Liam, his face lighting up greedily.

I grinned back at Nadima. '*Chocolate* Turkish Delight? Now that is an *inspired* idea!'

38

Chocolate Turkish Delight

For the next three evenings we turned Nadima's kitchen into a Chocolate Turkish Delight factory. I went round on the Monday night to help make the first batch.

I hadn't seen her mum since the family-tree homework. I wasn't sure if I should mention it. I could hardly say, 'I'm sorry about all your family who died in Syria,' could I? But then on the other hand, I couldn't just pretend it hadn't happened either. So when her mum came to the door I sort of stood there awkwardly. 'Um . . .' I said. Not my best opening line, I'll admit. She must have guessed what was going through my mind because pulled me into a warm hug. And then she sort of squeezed my arms before she let me go.

D'you know what? Sometimes, when you don't

know what to say, it's best not to say anything at all.

So then Nadima and I went through to the kitchen, made three tins of Turkish Delight and left it all to set overnight.

On the Tuesday evening we cut Monday's batch into chunks and dipped them in melted chocolate. Then we left them to cool on plates, while we made more. When the chocolate had set we all tasted a piece and . . . OMG it was AMAZING!!!

Even Nadima's mum was impressed. 'You can be cook, like me!' she said to me.

I laughed. 'What about Nadima?' I asked.

Her mum smiled and shook her head. 'Doctor.'

'You want to be a doctor?' I asked Nadima.

She nodded.

I couldn't imagine anyone else in 7R wanting to be a doctor. Or possibly in the whole of Year 7 – and to be honest, it would be an utterly terrifying thought if they did. And there was no way I'd want to be one – I hate the sight of blood and I only have to get a whiff of upchuck and I start puking everywhere.

'You? For work?' she asked.

'I am going to run my own business and become a millionaire by the time I'm twenty-one,' I told her. She pulled her *I haven't got a clue what you're talking about* face, so I said, 'I am going to be rich!'

She grinned. 'Is good plan!'

By Wednesday evening you couldn't move in Nadima's kitchen for Turkish Delight. Every surface was covered.

Nadima's dad came home, did a comedy face-palm and pretended to reel backwards in shock.

'Is Turkish Delight everywhere!' he joked. 'Is like shop! Is like home!' Then he fled, laughing, into the living room, with Nadima's mum, leaving Nadima and me dunking chunks of Turkish Delight in melted chocolate.

'What was your home like?' I asked Nadima. 'In Syria, I mean.'

Nadima smiled and gave a small shrug. 'Was nice.'

'Do you have a photo of it?'

'No. No photo.'

My house is on Google Maps. I know because we checked. You can literally set the little man down outside our front garden. I was about to ask Nadima if hers was on Google Maps too. But I was worried that it might have been bombed. And there might be nothing left but a big pile of rubble – like you see on the news. Imagine if your home, and everything you had, was smashed to smithereens. Just a pile of rubble and dust.

It was a terrible thought – and I couldn't ask her outright, could I? So I said, 'Did you have a big house?'

She shook her head.

'Not house. Flat. Everyone have flat. Only rich have house.'

'You weren't very rich then?'

'Not rich!' She laughed.

'Were you poor?'

'No!' she exclaimed, shocked. 'Sweet shop very good! Not poor!'

Then her face sort of fell a bit and she went on, 'But here, here we poor. Here we have . . . not much.'

I wished there was something I could do to help them. But my allowance wasn't going to make much of a difference, was it?

'It must be hard,' I said.

'Yes. Is hard. But we are safe.' She brightened and added, 'We have new home now.'

'And you have me!' I said.

'Huh!' She rolled her eyes and shoved a bit of Chocolate Turkish Delight in my mouth.

39

Special Delivery

On Thursday morning Mum dropped us off at school. I'd brought everything we needed for the stall. Food bags, money for change, a huge banner to stick on the wall behind us and some Blu Tak. We'd decided to call our stall 'Sweet Treats'. Fyi, the name was Kara's idea. But it was a good one, so I wasn't going to let that get in the way. I'd spent hours on the computer making flyers to pin round the school, and I'd printed off loads, which The Brothers had promised to help stick up. By break-time the whole school was going to be *plastered* with them! I'd made the banner on the back of a couple of old posters I'd begged off Dan. It was pretty impressive, if I say so myself. Well, it was massive. And that was the main thing.

*

I suddenly realised I'd left Nadima to cope with lugging all the Turkish Delight in on her own. So I went to look for her at the school gates . . . and there she was, dragging a large holdall on wheels behind her.

She grinned and waved. 'Delivery!' she cried. 'Special delivery!'

Honestly, how does she even pick up English just like that? It's like she only has to hear something once and she can remember it.

By the time we'd hauled the bag into our form room, the others had arrived. Kara had a cake tin full of Rocky Road and Ryan had a tub of his nan's Peppermint Creams. They took one look at the enormous holdall and their chins hit the floor!

'Whoooa!' exclaimed Ryan. 'How much have you brought?!'

'Is lots!' laughed Nadima, unzipping the bag. It was crammed full.

'Oh, that's ridiculous!' Kara snapped. 'We'll never sell all that!'

'Wanna bet?' I replied.

'There's tons of it!' said Lily.

'Let's try some?' begged Liam, coming over.

Nadima took out a bag, tore it open, and offered everyone in our team a chunk.

Ryan bit into his and rolled his eyes in pleasure. 'Mmmm! MORE!' he cried.

So then *everyone* in 7R swooped in like greedy seagulls.

'No chance! You'll have to buy it – after lunch. 50p a bag!' I laughed, zipping up the holdall.

'Still think we won't sell it all?' I asked Kara.

She didn't reply.

Straight after lunch on Thursday we all shot into the hall to grab a good table and set up the stall.

I got out the banner, unrolled it and went to stick it to the wall behind our table when Kara suddenly exploded at me.

'What's that supposed to say!' she screeched, flicking her hair.

'Sweet Treats!' I replied. 'That's what we decided to call it – remember?' I added witheringly.

'That's not how you spell "treats"!' she cried. 'You've put two "e"s instead of "e-a"! You've spelt it wrong!'

I looked at the banner and my heart sank. She was right. I'd put 'SWEET TREETS'.

'It doesn't matter,' Lily was saying. But I hardly heard her. My face and ears were burning so hot.

I was gutted. Why hadn't I got one of The Brothers to check my spelling? WHY?!? I *know* I can't spell to save my life. IDIOT!!! I wanted the ground to swallow me up there and then. And even worse, The Brothers had plastered my flyers *everywhere* – and they were all spelt wrong too! So the entire school would know I couldn't spell.

I wanted to die.

'You can't put it up,' announced Kara. 'I'm not having everyone think we can't even spell the name of our own stall!'

But Nadima suddenly said, 'Kara! Is not mistake! Is Jaz make joke. Is funny, like "Toys 'R' Us"!'

'Oh, yeah! It's neat!' said Lily. Then she and Nadima helped me stick the banner up. I could have hugged both of them.

I left the others piling sweets onto paper plates and wandered round the hall to check out the opposition from the other stalls.

Not everyone in our year had a stall, of course. Lots of the groups were raising money doing other things. But even so, it was pretty rubbish.

There were only about ten of them. They mostly fell into two types:

a) geeky boys running cringingly lame 'fantasy' games for 50p a go, and
b) girls' stalls.

Chloe and Elly's group were doing French plaits and fishtail braids and stuff for £1. I watched Chloe doing a waterfall braid on Elly. It was very complicated – so they weren't going to do that many in the two hours we'd been given, were they?

Some of the girls from 7T were selling handmade jewellery. But it was mostly just friendship bracelets and beaded stuff. And there were three (*three!*) stalls selling cupcakes.

So it didn't look like competition was very fierce. We just had to hope Nad's *killer* combo of chocolate *and* Turkish delight would be a massive hit.

It was.

OMG.

We were mobbed.

The sweets literally flew off the stall – it was way more popular than Kara's Rocky Road. Some of the kids even came back for another bag and lots of them asked where we'd got it.

'Nadima and I made it!' I told them proudly, flinging my arm around Nadima.

They were well impressed. Nad tried to look modest, but I could see she was really thrilled.

So I added, 'It was Nadima's idea – and her mum's recipe.'

It was the chocolate that did it. Nobody seemed to care what was inside. In fact hardly anyone even bothered to ask. It was crazy – especially when you think about the time we tried selling ordinary Turkish Delight, when everyone behaved like we were trying to flog them sugared slugs or something.

By the end of our session, there was nothing left except a few of Ryan's nan's Peppermint Creams.

'Should have got your nan to cover them in chocolate,' said Lily drily, and we all laughed – even Kara.

40

ℰ Nadima's Family ℰ

At the end of the afternoon on Friday, we all trooped into the hall for a whole-school assembly where the winners of the Charity Challenge were to be announced. Butterflies were turning somersaults in my stomach. We'd already worked out we were the winning team in Year 7 – but I wanted to be the best team in the *entire* school.

Some local bigwig had been dragged in to read out the results and hand out the book tokens. He stood on the stage, confronted by fifteen hundred bored faces. Bravely he tried to make the occasion exciting – mostly by reading out the three winning teams in reverse order and leaving a lot of dramatic pauses. Well, I suppose it works on TV.

'The overall winners of this year's Charity Challenge are . . .' (long pause) '. . . in third place . . .' (another long pause) '. . . The Karaoke Kings from Year 8!'

There was a smattering of polite applause – mostly from the teachers.

'In second place . . .' (longer pause) '. . . The Fantasy Cupcake Bakers from Year 10!' This got a few whoops from some of the Year 10 girls. Probably the Fantasy Cupcake Bakers themselves. My hands had gone all sweaty, and my mouth was dry.

'But in first place . . .' (annoyingly long pause) '. . . this year's Charity Challenge winners are . . .' (*excruciatingly long* pause*) '. . . Sweet Treets from Year 7!'

Kara squealed, Liam and Ryan high-fived and the whole of 7R burst out cheering and clapping. Nadima and I threw our arms around each other, nearly crushing each other to death! Then we all went up onstage to collect our book tokens. At the back of the hall Matt gave me a big thumbs up. He looked dead proud, and I couldn't stop grinning. I stood there, beaming with pride. But most of all I was really, really looking forward to what was going to happen next.

Remember I said the winning team got to nominate the local charity that would get all the money raised? Well, Ryan and Liam had said they didn't care, and Kara and Lily didn't know any local charities, so I'd made the decision myself without discussing it with anyone.

It was meant to be a brilliant surprise.

As it turned out, it was a disaster. A total disaster.

The bigwig held up the piece of paper with the charity's name on.

'Well, I've not heard of this organisation,' he said, frowning, 'but I'm sure it's a good one! The charity that's going to receive *all* the money raised in this year's Charity Challenge is . . .' and he did the dramatic pause thing again, before announcing, '. . . Nadima's Family!'

I'd imagined this moment in my head, over and over again. A huge cheer going up and a massive grateful hug from Nadima.

That's *so* not what happened.

Nadima gasped and there was a stunned silence. Then everyone either called out things like, 'That's not fair,' or, worse, burst out laughing.

'It *is* fair, and it's not *funny*!' I shouted, furiously. 'Don't you people even watch the news?' I thundered. 'Nadima's family are from Syria. They're refugees and they had to leave *everything* behind when they came here. Back home they had a shop

213

and a business and everything, but here, they have nothing. They're poor, and they need the money.'

At which point Nadima burst into tears and rushed off the stage.

'Nadima!' I cried, shooting off after her.

'Nad! What is it? What's wrong!' I called, catching up with her in the corridor.

'Why you do that? Why you say that?' she shouted, turning on me angrily. Her fists were clenched and for a moment I thought she was going to hit me. Tears of rage spilled down her cheeks. 'We not poor. We proud,' she yelled. Then, because even now her English wasn't up to really explaining how she felt, she resorted to a stream of Kurdish.

I couldn't understand the words – but I understood the emotions – and the volume. Especially the volume. Eventually she stopped bawling at me in Kurdish and said, 'You shame me. You shame my family. You not my friend.' Then she fled along the corridor in tears.

I stood there feeling completely numb. I couldn't believe what had just happened. Then the bell went for end of school and everyone starting pouring out of the hall. I couldn't face seeing anyone, so I ran. I raced down the corridor and out of the building, and I kept on running until I got to the pick-up area where all the school buses were lined up. I dived onto our bus and slid into one of the back seats, where Matt always sits with his sixth-form mates. I sat there with my knees hunched up, waiting for him, and hoping he'd let me hide there for the journey home.

41

Hiding, Again

I couldn't face telling Mum what had happened so I asked Matt to.

'Sure,' he said, giving me a big hug. I thought The Brothers would be angry with me for embarrassing them in front of the whole school. Or tease me for making a fool of myself. But they didn't. They were lovely to me. And so was Mum, when she got home. Which all made it even worse – because then I knew how *spectacularly* badly I'd messed up.

After supper Mum came up to my room and sat down on the bed.

'Do you want to talk?' she asked.

'Not really,' I said. So she went off and came back with a tub of salted caramel ice cream and two spoons. Then she sat next to me and we worked our way slowly down the tub.

A storm of texts pinged into my phone. I went to answer them, but Mum firmly took the phone off me and turned it off. Then she put it in her back pocket.

'Are you punishing me?' I asked.

'No, I'm protecting you,' she replied. 'I think it's probably a good idea if you lie low for a day or two.'

I slobbed around miserably all weekend, in my PJs, watching stuff on YouTube, endless cartoons and romcoms, trying to cheer myself up. Nothing worked. I kept going over and over what had happened. Not during assembly. I wasn't bothered about looking stupid in front of everyone. I only cared about what had gone wrong with Nadima. I honestly couldn't work out why she was so angry with me. I kept seeing her tearful face yelling at me, 'We not poor. We proud.' And telling me I'd 'shamed' her and her family.

But they *are* poor. She'd told me so herself. And anyhow, there's nothing wrong with being poor. It's nothing to be ashamed of. It's not like it's their fault. They're refugees. All refugees are poor – because they have to leave almost everything behind. Didn't they want the money? I just didn't get it.

*

Late on Sunday afternoon Mum came up to dump a pile of clean school uniform on my bed.

'Have you got any homework?' she asked.

Fyi, I didn't know and I didn't care. But I didn't think it would be a good idea to say that, so I said, 'I'll check,' and hauled my school bag onto my bed.

She sort of hovered in the doorway. 'Why don't you come downstairs for a while? Watch a movie? Play a game?'

I shook my head. 'I'm not in the mood.' She didn't push it.

I dug around in my bag for my planner and flicked through to it check for homework. There was some maths – but it didn't need to be done until Tuesday. Then I remembered I'd meant to redo my family tree – but leaving my dad off it. So I got out my history book. I was just about to rip the page out, but I suddenly couldn't be bothered to do the whole thing all over again. Maybe I should just leave it with his name crossed out? Or, better still . . . I grabbed the Tippex out of the top drawer of my desk, and carefully covered over his name. Completely. Mrs B would probably just think it was a mistake. There was no way she'd guess the truth. Not that it mattered if she did.

I stuck my finger on the Tippex to make sure it was dry. It was. Then I scanned the family tree and realised Mum was right. Without my dad's name it *did* look like she'd had four kids without even being married! It was a good job she wouldn't care about that. Besides, bringing us lot up single-handed was something to be proud of – not ashamed.

And then it hit me.

Nadima wasn't *ashamed* about her family being poor. She wasn't ashamed of them *at all*. She was proud of her family. Proud of how Rasha and Sami were learning English. Proud her mum was such a brilliant cook. Proud that her dad had been a successful businessman. Proud of her family's sweet shop.

And now, like a complete and utter idiot, I'd gone and told the *entire* school they were so poor that they needed charity. Like a homeless person or a street beggar. That's how I'd 'shamed' her. I wanted to curl up and die.

There was no way I could undo that. Or put it right. How was I ever going to be able to make it up to Nadima?

42

Tears

I don't know how I found the guts to go in to school on Monday. I was totally dreading it. As I walked towards our form block I could see Lily and everyone in a huddle round Nadima. But long before I reached them, Lily broke away and came up to me.

'Nadima asked me to give you this,' she said, handing me the pink and silver BFF bracelet. I shoved it in my bag and then slipped off to the girls' loos, locked myself in a cubicle and sobbed and sobbed.

It got worse.

Mrs C called me out of registration, took me to her office and treated me to a full lecture.

'Jaz, you have been incredibly insensitive and tactless. You've treated Nadima as if she was one of your "campaigns" or a school project!' she told me.

'I was trying to help them,' I said quietly. 'They're refugees – they need our help.'

'But not like that! There's a difference between giving them support and making them feel like a charity case. You insulted her family! In front of the entire school.'

'I know. I'm sorry,' I said. I bit my lip and to my horror felt tears sting my eyes.

I think Mrs C was surprised I wasn't arguing back at her like I usually do. Because then she started being nice to me, which made it even worse.

'Jaz, you're not insensitive and you're not stupid. You're a lovely, kind, bright girl and you absolutely have your heart in the right place. I think it's wonderful the way you and Nadima have overcome a huge language difficulty and become friends. I really do.'

I burst into tears. She handed me a tissue.

'But you *must* stop charging in like a bull in a china shop. It's good to want to help people, but you mustn't assume people need you to fight their battles for them. Especially when you're only a twelve-year-old girl and they're adults. And particularly this family – who have confronted and survived more terrible problems and disasters than you can begin to imagine. Most of all they need our friendship and support – not our charity.'

I nodded. I couldn't speak.

She got me a cup of tea and let me sit in her office until the bell went.

I headed off to geography. Up ahead of me in the corridor, Nadima was walking between Lily and Kara. Elly and Chloe were walking behind them. They were all laughing. I wanted to go up to Nadima and ask if we could talk. But I couldn't get near her. So I left it until we could talk in class. But in the lesson, Mr K told us to get into groups of four to design a weather station.

Kara's hand immediately shot up. 'Sir, can we be a five so that Nadima isn't left out?' she asked.

'Yes, good idea,' he said.

So guess who was left out? You do the sums. I ended up with Ryan and Liam and a couple of other boys.

I was desperate to talk to Nadima. So when the lesson ended and everyone was going out, I went up and put my hand on her arm.

'Nadima?' I said.

She turned to look at me. The others stopped

just behind her and stood watching, so I added, 'Can I talk to you?'

I thought the others would be tactful enough to drift off. Fat chance. Kara even pushed closer.

'Yes?' asked Nadima, politely.

'I just wanted to say sorry,' I mumbled.

She gave me a quick nod. 'OK. Yes. Thank you.' Then she went off with Kara and everyone, and just left me standing there.

43

Kara

Let's just say that school wasn't the most *enjoyable* place for the next week or so. Nadima was now totally one of Kara's gang. They didn't *exactly* exclude me. But I didn't feel comfortable being with them. So I started hanging round with Liam and Ryan. There are other girls in 7R (obviously), but to be honest I was happier being with the boys. Comes of having The Brothers, I suppose. Nadima didn't *ignore* me. But she didn't try to start a conversation – or tell me anything the way she used to.

Sometimes we were *forced* to talk to each other. Like in drama. We tried to sort of plot a basic storyline for stealing the Crown Jewels – which I drew, like a cartoon. But it was a rubbish idea to start with and it's not like either of us could actually write the story down, is it? So our drama lessons

224

were a complete waste of time. But then, what was new about that?

So school wasn't exactly a joy – but it was bearable – until the Wednesday of the second week.

Kara came bouncing into class first thing, before registration, and announced to *everyone* that she was having a sleepover on Saturday night.

'Brilliant! Can I come?' grinned Ryan.

'No! It's girls only!' snapped Kara.

'That's discrimination!' announced Liam.

She ignored him, but then, with a gobsmacking lack of tact, she handed out invitations to every single girl in the class except (yup, you've guessed it) me.

Then she came over and, pulling a 'sad face', she said in a big, loud voice, 'Jaz, I'm really sorry about this. I would invite you, you know I would, but I don't think I can invite both you *and* Nadima – and it would be really mean to exclude her, wouldn't it?'

Lily looked like she wanted the ground to swallow her up. The rest of the class were busy shooting sneaky glances in my direction to see how I'd take it.

So I just looked Kara straight in the eye and said

loudly, 'No, it's fine! I completely understand. Of course you should invite Nadima.'

Kara gave me one of those fake *aren't you lovely?* kind of grimaces and said, 'Thank you,' before flouncing off and sitting back down next to Nadima. Nadima looked over at me . . . but I looked away, burning hot and horribly aware of how red I'd gone.

'Are you OK?' asked Lily, when she sat down next to me for registration.

'Course I am! Why would I want to go to Kara's party anyway?' I replied.

I managed to put a brave face on it all day, but as soon as Mum got home I dissolved like chocolate in a microwave. I slumped over the kitchen table and bawled my eyes out.

'Oh, come on, sweetie,' Mum sighed, putting her arm round me. 'Try not to let it upset you.'

The Brothers rallied round of course.

'Sounds like that Kara's a ghastly piece of work,' said Matt, slopping out some spag bol into a bowl for me. (Wednesday – his turn to cook.)

'Horrible!' agreed Dan, through a mouthful of pasta.

226

'Loathsome and vile,' threw in Gus.

'Despicable, detestable and dreadful,' said Matt.

'Hideous, odious and horrible,' announced Gus.

'You can't have horrible, I've already said that,' said Dan.

'OK, Hideous, odious . . . and *obnoxious*!' said Gus.

'Oh, good one, Gus!' said Mum.

'I thank you!' said Gus, and then he shoved a forkful of spag bol into his mouth, deliberately slurping up a single strand of spaghetti so that he plastered his chin with sauce, trying to make me laugh. It didn't work.

'Come on, Jaz – man up!' he mumbled.

'Yeah!' said Dan, pretending to give me a super-slow-motion punch to the jaw.

'All the girls in our class fell out in Year 7,' said Matt. 'Nobody was talking to anybody and you needed a degree in diplomacy to make it through break. I don't think they started talking to each other again until Year 10.'

'Must've been lovely and quiet,' said Dan.

'Bliss!' Matt grinned.

'Huh, girls!' exclaimed Gus, rolling his eyes. 'The most toxic life form on planet earth!'

'Oi, what about me?' I protested.

'You're not a girl. You're an honorary Brother,' replied Gus.

Which made me laugh.

'Attagirl!' said Mum.

44

Lily

You'll never guess what happened the following day. Kara only came up to me and handed me an invitation to her sleepover!

I looked at it suspiciously. 'Did your mum say you had to invite me or something?'

'No, she did not! And you don't have to come if you don't want to,' she snapped, and she took it back. Then she flicked her hair and went over to sit on the table with Lily and Nadima and the others. So of course they instantly started talking about me. I couldn't hear what they were saying, but they kept shooting little glances my way. I ignored them.

A few moments later, Lily slid into the seat next to me and handed me the invitation again. 'I asked Kara to invite you,' she said.

I was gobsmacked. 'Why?'

'Because I want you to come, you muppet!' She grinned.

'You might, but nobody else does,' I muttered, glancing over to Kara and that lot. They were chatting away, pretending that they weren't trying to listen to every word we said.

'Jaz, that's not true.'

I started picking away at a blob of dried glue on the tabletop. 'Yes, it is. No one's hardly spoken to me at all for two weeks.'

'Well, you've hardly spoken to any of us either!' Lily put the invitation down on the table in front of me. 'I hate it like this, Jaz,' she said. 'It's horrible. Why can't we all just be friends like before.'

'Because it's not as simple as that, is it?' I said.

'Yes, it is! You're the one making it difficult.'

ME making it difficult? I nearly choked. 'No, I'm not! I'm not the one having a party and inviting everyone except me! So how is it my fault?'

'Well, you *have* been invited now,' said Lily, pushing the envelope towards me.

'Only because of you. Kara doesn't really want me there, does she? Or Nadima,' I pointed out.

I glanced over to Nadima, but when she saw me looking at her she blushed and looked away.

'How do you know Nadima doesn't want you there? Have you asked her?' said Lily.

I didn't answer. I just rolled my eyes.

'Please come, Jaz. Then maybe you and Nadima can have a chance to make up and we can all start being friends again.' She picked up the invitation and handed it to me again. 'Please?'

I didn't answer. I just took the envelope and stuffed it into my bag.

'I think you should go,' said Mum, when I showed her the invitation.

'You are joking! Wild unicorns wouldn't drag me to Kara's sleepover.'

We were unpacking the supermarket delivery. Gus and Dan were lugging the bags from the front door and dumping them on the kitchen table, while Mum and I put the stuff away.

'If you don't go you'll just make things worse,' said Mum, loading vegetables into the fridge. 'Look, Kara's made a gesture of friendship by inviting you. Accept it, and go!'

'But *she* doesn't really want me to go. Lily made her invite me,' I said, slamming a multipack of baked beans into the cupboard with a satisfying crash.

231

'Even more reason for you to go then,' said Mum. 'Lily really wants to stay friends with you – so don't make it harder for her!'

'What about Nadima? What if she doesn't want me there?'

'It's not her party so it's not her choice,' said Gus, taking a packet of chocolate biscuits out of one of the bags and opening it. He handed me one.

'Come on, Jaz! Think this through. Don't cut off your nose to spite your face!' said Mum.

'Oh, I dunno. Might be an improvement if she did,' said Dan.

I grinned and made a rude sign at him behind Mum's back.

In the end I decided to go. But only for Lily's sake.

45

Sleepover

Matt drove me to Kara's sleepover. As we pulled up outside her house I nearly chickened out.

'If everyone's horrible to me, you will come and get me, won't you?' I said.

'Yup. You can call International Rescue any time!' he joked, in a terrible American accent. Then he added in his own voice, 'But you won't need to. It'll be fine.' So I gathered up my sleeping bag and pillow, my overnight bag and my courage, and headed in.

I'd never been to Kara's house before. It's dead modern and quite big. Bigger than ours anyway. Just as well, since she'd literally invited *all* the girls in our class. I was one of the last to arrive, and by the time I'd got there the kitchen was full of people all chattering away and helping themselves to Coke and pizza and stuff.

When Kara saw me hovering in the hall she yelled, 'Dump your stuff in the living room!' and pointed. So I did. Then I went to find Lily. She was dancing with Nadima and the others in the conservatory. The music was OFF THE SCALE! Kara's phone was plugged into these *huge* speakers and the noise literally bounced round the room, along with the multicoloured flashes from the disco lights. Lily's face lit up when she saw me, and she pulled me over to dance with them. Nadima carried on dancing and messing around with Chloe and Elly. They were pretending Elle's Coke can was a mic and singing away and laughing their heads off. Honestly, you'd think Nadima had known everyone *forever*, the way she just fitted in.

After a while we all went off to get a drink. It was much quieter, and cooler, in the kitchen. But it was still pretty crowded and I ended up shoved in a corner, with Nadima.

It was the perfect chance to talk to her – and to try to make up. So I smiled at her and she smiled back. But I suddenly couldn't think of anything to say. I couldn't remember all the things we used to talk about. All I could think to say was, 'It's a good party, isn't it?' (Groan. How lame was that?)

She nodded. 'Yes.'

'The music's a bit loud though!'

'Yes,' she said. 'Is very loud.'

After that I couldn't think of anything to say. And she didn't say anything to me. So we stood there awkwardly, until Kara came and dragged Nad off to dance.

Well, I'd tried. I tried talking to her and she was polite, but she wasn't friendly like she used to be. You can't *make* someone be friends with you, can you? If she didn't want to be friends any more then that was her choice.

I suddenly wanted to go home. I got my phone out to call International Rescue but just then Lil grabbed me.

'Come on!' she squealed. 'You love this song!' and she dragged me back into the conservatory to dance. So I stayed, because I didn't want to upset Lily.

After it had got properly dark, Kara's stepdad called everyone out onto the patio.

'Stay by the house!' he yelled, heading off down the garden.

'What's going on?' Kara asked him. 'What are you doing?'

'It's a surprise!' he called. We clustered round, giggling excitedly. Seconds later he came back to stand next to us, and then, all of a sudden . . . WHOOSH, sparkle, sparkle! A row of Roman candles burst into life, against the back fence. Silver and purple sparkles fizzed and cracked, brittle and bright.

'Ooooooh!' we all cried.

He'd bought one of those big tubs of fireworks where you only have to light one fuse and they all go off one after the other. It must've cost a fortune! He obviously wanted the sleepover to be a big hit, no matter what Kara thought of him.

WHOOOOSH! A rocket suddenly shot up into the dark and then . . . BANG! it exploded, scattering coloured sparks against the sky. We all screamed and clung to each other, pretending to be scared.

Except Nadima.

She screamed. But then she carried on screaming, and screaming and screaming, with her hands pressed against her face and her eyes wide with terror.

WHOOOSH . . . BANG!

Another rocket went off.

Nadima turned and fled into the house.

46
Home

'Nadima!' I went racing after her.

She charged through the kitchen, knocking over a stool and nearly falling over but she didn't seem to even notice. She just lurched on blindly into the living room.

'Nadima! Nad!' I cried. But it was as if she couldn't hear me. Panic-stricken, she looked around wildly as if she had no idea where she was.

'Basement! Where is basement?' she cried.

'There isn't a basement!' I said.

Sobbing, she flung herself behind the sofa. The others had all rushed in behind me by now. Outside, the fireworks carried on their dazzling fizzing and flashing, booming and banging – but there was no one there to enjoy them.

Kara's mum pushed forward, through the cluster of girls, trying to take control.

'What's going on?' she asked. 'Who's that behind the sofa?'

'It's Nadima,' said Kara. 'I think she's frightened of fireworks.'

Everyone stood in a confused huddle, not knowing what to do.

Every time there was another BOOM or FLASH from the fireworks Nadima cried out in fear.

Kara's mum leaned over the back of the sofa. 'Nadima. It's fine. There's nothing to be frightened of. Fireworks can't hurt you,' she said.

Nadima didn't answer. We could hear her sobbing hysterically.

'She doesn't speak much English,' I said.

'Should we call her parents?' asked Kara's stepdad.

'They don't speak English either,' I said.

Kara's mum and stepdad exchanged horrified looks while everyone else just stood there helplessly, not knowing what to do. Then Kara's mum tried to pull the sofa away from the wall, but that set Nadima off screaming again.

'Leave the sofa,' I said, and I dropped to my knees and crawled in behind it to join Nadima. She was curled up with her hands over her head, crying and trembling.

'Nad, it's me. It's me, Jaz,' I said, and I put my arms round her. But she just kept on crying. She was shaking all over. So I just kept hugging her and repeating, 'It's OK. It's safe. It's OK.' I made sure I said everything as simply as possible so she could understand.

She grabbed hold of me. 'Is not OK. Is bombs. Is bullets. Everywhere. Is not OK.'

I concentrated on speaking calmly and clearly. 'No. It's not bombs. It's not bullets. It's fireworks. Only fireworks. No bombs, no bullets here. You're safe.'

She clung to me and eventually, once the display had finally stopped, she calmed down. I helped her scramble out from behind the sofa.

'Are you all right?' asked Kara's mum, her face full of concern.

Nadima nodded.

'Why would she think it was bombs and bullets?' Kara's stepdad asked me in a shocked voice.

'She's from Syria. Her family only arrived a short while ago,' I said.

Kara's mum's hand flew to her mouth. 'Kara! Why didn't you tell me? We would *never* have had fireworks if we'd known,' she exclaimed.

'I didn't know we were having fireworks!' protested Kara. She looked close to tears.

Kara's mum turned to me. 'Does she want to go home?' she asked.

I looked questioningly at Nadima. She shook her head. 'No. Not home. Is late. Mum and Dad be scared. Not home.' Then she looked at me pleadingly. 'Your home? Please?'

'Of course,' I said. 'Yes.'

Lily and Kara gathered up our overnight stuff and I phoned Mum to come and fetch us.

By the time we got home, Matt had blown up the air mattress and put it on the floor in my room for Nadima. She had her own quilt and pillow, from the sleepover, but I made her take my bed and I bunked down on the floor.

'Please can have light on?' she said.

'OK,' I said, switching the bedside lamp on. 'All right?'

She nodded. Then she sat, leaning against the wall, with my quilt wrapped round her and started talking . . . and talking . . . and talking. She wanted to explain why the fireworks had panicked her.

'Is like bombs. Bombs and guns. Flash and bang, flash and *crack-crack-crack*!'

And she began to tell me what it had been like, back home in Syria, living in the middle of a war. You know, the one we see every night on the news – from the safety of our living rooms. The one that's hundreds of miles away from us so it doesn't really bother us. The one that's killed loads and loads of people – mums and dads, and brothers and sisters, and aunts and uncles, and cousins and little kids and babies. The one we've stopped being shocked by. That one.

'Is all time. Is every day. Every night,' she said. 'Boom, flash, BOOM. Screaming. Crying. BANG and then CRASH. Building fall down. People dead. Bang and flash and guns, *crack-crack*. People dead. No one safe. Building hit. Is glass, cut face, cut hands, cut eyes, can't walk without cut feet. People dead.'

I began to understand how terrifying it was to

be bombed and shot at, day after day after day, night after night. And to find your neighbours or your family had been crushed under their homes, or your teacher had been blown up by a bomb, or your friend had been shot dead. And all the time being terrified that it would be you next or your mum and dad. Or Rasha or little Sami.

'Bombs come. We go to basement. We hide. Mum, Dad, Rasha and Sami and me. We curl up. Sami in middle. Wait for bombs to stop. All people from flats are in basement.

'We cannot go out. Is not safe. But is no food. No water. My dad go. We beg him stay. We think he not come back.

'Then *crack-crack*. Is guns. Is he OK? We not know! We wait. We wait. We hope.

'Is men in street with guns. Shooting, shooting. And is no school. Bomb school. Bomb shop. Bomb hospital. Is nowhere safe.

She hugged her knees, tears streaming silently down her face.

I climbed onto the bed and pulled her into a hug.

'You're safe now,' I told her. 'You're all safe now.'

She closed her eyes and more tears spilled out.

She shook her head. 'We safe. But Ishtar? Baby Amira? Jamal?'

I didn't know what to say. I just sat with her until she finally stopped crying and drifted off to sleep. I think she was exhausted.

47

Kurdish for BFFs

We slept late the next morning. Mum told us to have a lie-in and she brought us up some breakfast – OJ and chocolate spread on toast. She told Nadima not to get up if she didn't feel like it. But Nadima said she was OK, and then she texted her parents to tell them where she was. So Mum offered to go round to Nadima's to tell them what had happened.

'NO!' cried Nadima. She didn't want her parents to worry.

But Mum put on her 'responsible adult' face and said she was sorry, but she had to tell them. Otherwise how would Nadima explain why she was at our house rather than Kara's?

When Mum had left the room, Nadima said, 'You are good friend, Jaz.'

I wished it was true. I wished I was a better

friend. The sort of friend that hadn't embarrassed her, and shamed her family, in front of the *entire* school.'

'About the Charity Challenge . . .' I started to say. But she cut me off.

'Is OK, Jaz. You were just try to be nice. To help us. I know.' Then she added sheepishly, 'Please can have . . . ?' and she circled her wrist with the fingers of her other hand.

'Your bracelet?' I smiled.

'Yes, *bracelet*,' she repeated.

I pulled it out from the bottom of my school bag where I'd shoved it when Lily had given it to me. Nad held out her wrist and I tied it on her. I put mine back on too.

She pointed to the letters on the heart. 'What mean?' she asked.

'Best friends forever,' I reminded her.

'Best friends forever,' she repeated.

Then she decided to teach me how to say it in Kurdish! So she typed 'best friends forever' into her phone and showed me the screen:

> hevalê baş ê her dêmê

'Seriously, Nadima?!' I snorted. 'There's no way I can say that!'

'Yes!' She grinned, and she read it out for me to repeat – knowing full well there was no way I could even get beyond the first word!

Just then there was a knock at the front door. I heard Mum answer it and then say, 'Yes, go on up.' Then she shouted, 'Kara's here.'

I shot a surprised look at Nadima. Kara's *never* even been to my house before.

I heard her feet on the stairs and then she stopped on the landing, not knowing which room was mine. So I opened my door.

'Hi,' she said awkwardly, standing in the doorway.

'Hi,' I said.

She carried on. 'I just wanted to come round and say sorry to Nadima, for upsetting her.' And then she surprised me even more by adding, 'Um, and to thank you for . . . you know, for looking after her.'

We stood there looking at each other for a moment. Then she held out a carrier bag. 'You missed the midnight feast, so I brought you some popcorn.'

'Thank you,' I said, taking the bag. I stood back to let her into my room. Then I went and sat back down on my bed, next to Nadima. Kara sort of hovered in the middle of the room.

'Come and sit down,' I said. So she sat cross-legged on the air mattress.

There was a bit of a silence, while I ripped open the popcorn and offered it to her.

'Thanks,' she said, taking a small handful.

We all sat munching popcorn for a while, until Kara said, 'I was *sooo* worried about you, Nadima,' as *melodramatically* as ever, I noted. 'I'm really sorry about the fireworks. You must have been *terrified*!'

I wondered if she'd come round for a bit more drama. But maybe I was being unfair, because then she looked at me and said, 'My mum was dead impressed by you, Jaz. I don't know what would have happened if you hadn't been there.'

I shrugged. 'I was only looking out for Nad.'

'Well, thank you anyway,' she said. There was a pause and then she started to get up as if she was leaving.

'You can stay for a bit, if you like,' I offered.

'Actually, my mum's outside in the car,' she said.

'Can't she come back later?' I asked.

I watched her face as she decided what to do. It went from surprise, to confusion, and then settled in a smile and she said, 'OK. Thanks. ' She texted her mum and settled back down. So I offered her some more popcorn.

We listened to music, chatted a bit and worked our way down the bag of popcorn. She didn't stay long because she had to go and help clear up after last night. When she left she hugged Nadima, and then she hugged me. So I hugged her back. It was a bit awkward, but it would have been rude not to, wouldn't it? Nad and I hung over the banisters as she went down the stairs.

'Thanks for coming to my party,' she called up.

'Thanks for inviting me,' I replied.

'Thanks for popcorn!' shouted Nadima with a grin.

'You're welcome!' called Kara, as she shut the front door.

After she'd gone, Nadima started helping me sort out the beds. She rolled her pillow up inside her quilt, neatly, 'Kara is nice, Jaz. You can be friends,' she said.

'No we can't. She doesn't like me really,' I said, letting the air mattress down.

'Is not true.' Nadima shook her head.

'It is. And she doesn't like me and Lily being friends.'

'Maybe she think Lily like you more than Lily like her.'

I stared at her. That *literally* hadn't occurred to me. I thought about it for a moment and then I said, 'Well, she's wrong. Lily likes Kara more than she likes me.'

Nadima burst out laughing.

'What's so funny?'

'You think Lily like Kara more than you. Kara think Lily like you more than Kara. But Lily like both of you!'

Then she spoke more slowly, like she was choosing her words and building her sentence carefully.

'Jaz, I think . . . I think you should try like Kara. If you like Kara, then maybe Kara like you. And everyone be friends.'

I thought about it. Maybe she had a point.

48
❧ Inspired! ❧

On Monday everything was much better at school. Now that Nadima and I had made up, the whole gang sort of gelled together again – without anyone having to worry about who was talking to who, or whatever. Even Kara was trying to be nice.

Nadima and I still had our dreaded drama storytelling hanging over us of course.

Everyone else was rehearsing or putting finishing touches to their presentations which we had to perform *the following Monday* (groan). But Nadima and I were still stuck struggling with the *ridonkulous* idea of making up a story around stealing the Crown Jewels.

I looked around in despair. Lily and Kara had already romped through their 'final' rehearsal. Lily caught my eye and they came over.

'How's it going?' she asked.

'Oh, don't even ask,' I groaned.

'Is not good!' said Nadima, pulling a face.

Lily laughed and shrugged. 'Don't worry about it! It's only a drama project!'

'Yeah, it's not going to be the end of the world if you mess it up,' said Kara.

I wondered if she was gloating. But then, much to my amazement, she offered to help us.

'What's your story about?' she added, suddenly looking all businesslike.

'Stealing the Crown Jewels.'

I could tell by her face she thought it was a totally rubbish idea. 'Right, um . . . well . . .' she said politely.

'It's a rubbish idea, isn't it?' I said.

'No, er . . . it could be . . . interesting,' she said carefully, until I told her it was Mrs P's idea, at which point she said, 'Yes, it's a totally rubbish idea!' and we both burst out laughing.

'OMG I can just imagine her!' Kara giggled, rolling her eyes and going off on a perfect impression of Mrs P: 'Yes, yes, yes! Stealing the Crown Jewels! It's a brilliant idea, girls! Brilliant, BRILLIANT!' she gushed. 'Honestly, the woman's an idiot!' she finished.

I grinned. Then I remembered what Nad had said yesterday, after Kara had gone. Something about 'if I liked Kara then maybe she would like me'. Come to think of it, it must have been a bit of a tough thing for Kara to do, coming round to mine. I bet her mum had made her do it. And it wasn't like she'd even been to my house before.

So I said, 'Oh, I meant to say thanks for coming round yesterday, Kara. It was nice of you.' Lily beamed at me.

Kara shrugged lightly. 'No problem. Thanks for inviting me in!' she said.

'You're welcome,' I said. And then I added, 'Any time,' and I thought Lily's face would literally crack in half, she was smiling so much.

Then Lily suggested we join in their presentation. 'They could just do the same as me,' she said to Kara. 'We wouldn't have to make up anything new.' I could see she was desperately hoping Kara would say yes.

We all looked at Kara. 'OK,' she said, and I could tell she was doing it for Lily.

So Kara went off to ask Mrs P. I bet she wouldn't say no to Kara. She never says no to Kara.

I was wrong.

Mrs P came sailing over, her enormous kaftan dazzling us all with its clashing colours. Kara trailed behind her, looking cross.

'Girls, girls, girls! It's absolutely *lovely* that you all want to be together, and I'm sure you'd all create something absolutely fabulous and brilliant together. Yes, brilliant! And I don't want to dampen your enthusiasm, or your creativity, but on this occasion I really do want Jaz and Nadima to tell their *own* story.' She pulled an apologetic face before shooing Kara and Lily off.

'Sorry,' mouthed Kara, with a shrug.

'Thanks for trying,' I said.

Nadima looked really disappointed. But I wasn't, because, and I can't believe I'm even saying this, Mrs P had given me the most *inspired* idea.

'Nadima, let's not do stealing the Crown Jewels,' I said.

'Yes. Is totally rubbish idea,' she agreed.

'Let's do *your* story instead.'

'My story?' She frowned.

'Not if you don't want to. I mean, we don't have to tell *your* story. But maybe one about a girl *like* you, and about what it was like for her living in Syria . . . and maybe we could add a bit about how she and her family got here. So not *your* story – but *her* story.'

'Not *my* story, *her* story?' she said, as if she was trying to sort out the two ideas in her head.

'Yes.'

She thought about it for a moment, and I was worried that she would be angry with me for suggesting it. But then a lovely slow smile spread across her face and deep into her eyes.

'No, not *her* story. *My* story,' she announced. 'We do *my* story.'

49
Nadima's Story

The following Monday morning, most of 7R dawdled into the drama studio with about as much enthusiasm as a bunch of zombies. Only Nadima and I (oh, and Kara of course) looked happy to be there. Mrs P put a large cardboard box in the middle of the floor.

'Don't forget to use *The Box*,' she trilled. 'It's our theme, remember.'

Then she asked who would like to volunteer to go first. Much to everyone's gobsmacked amazement, I put up my hand. 7R sat there, obviously bored to death, waiting to see what we were going to do.

They had absolutely no idea what was about to hit them.

Nadima lay down curled up on the floor at my feet and pretended to be asleep. I stood facing the class.

255

'Nadima's Story,' I announced and I held up a photo of her family I'd taken at the weekend. 'Once upon a time there was a family who lived in Syria. Mum, Dad, Nadima, Rasha and little Sami. One night, they were all fast asleep when suddenly . . .'

I dropped the photo, jumped up in the air and landed as loudly as I could right next to Nadima.

'*KA-BOOM!*' I yelled.

Nadima sat up and screamed.

Half the class nearly jumped out of their skins – and lots of the kids started laughing. We ignored them and carried on. I kept jumping round and round Nadima, landing as heavily as I could. 'KA-BOOM! . . . KA-BOOM! . . . KA-BOOM!'

Nadima flung her arms over her head and curled up into a ball.

'Bombs fell everywhere,' I said. 'KA-BOOM! One landed on the flats next door. KA-BOOM!'

And then I paused, before I said, 'All Nadima's neighbours died.'

At which point the kids stopped laughing.

Nadima got to her feet and held up a photo of a school.

'Nowhere was safe. KA-BOOM!' I went.

Nadima tore the picture in half and dropped the

pieces on the floor. Then she picked up a picture of a hospital.

'KA-BOOM!' I yelled.

Nadima tore up that picture too. As she dropped the pieces she said, 'Many people die.'

Then I pretended I had a gun and ran round 'shooting' everyone.

'Ak-kak-kak-kak-kak! Peyow! Peyow!'

'Is not safe outside. Soldiers shoot you,' said Nadima. Then she crouched down on the floor with her hands over her head.

'Nadima and her family hid in the basement,' I said. 'But soon they ran out of food and water. So her dad *had* to go out.'

Then Nadima stood up, and with her head high she said proudly, 'My dad very brave. Maybe he come back. Maybe he die. We hear bombs. We hear guns. We wait. We hope.'

By now the class were sitting wide-eyed and dead quiet. I paused before I said, 'Hours and hours later, he did come back. But he said that some of Nadima's aunties and uncles and her cousins had been killed.'

Kara's hand flew to her mouth, and lots of other girls did the same.

'Nadima's father said they had to leave, before they all died too,' I said.

Nadima knelt by the cardboard box, packing it with stuff she'd brought from home, including one of Rasha's little dresses, Sami's bunny onesie and his little fluffy blue teddy.

'We no can take much,' she said.

Then we held up a big map of Syria with the route Nadima's family had taken marked on it in red.

'We walk for four days,' said Nadima. 'Mum carry Rasha, Dad carry bag, I carry Sami. We get to refugee camp. But camp full. People say is dangerous.'

I held up a photo of a refugee camp made up of hundreds and hundreds of tents.

'Then a man told Nadima's dad he could get them on a boat to Europe. He took all their money and they had to get on a tiny boat with lots of others,' I said, holding up more photos. These ones showed refugees crammed into boats on the sea.

Nadima climbed into the cardboard box and sat hugging herself and looking scared. 'Is too many people. We afraid boat will sink. My family, we hold each other.'

'The sea got rough and the waves got higher and higher and water came into the boat. Everyone had to keep bailing – with their bare hands, otherwise the boat would sink. Nobody had a life jacket. Not even little Rasha or baby Sami,' I said.

Nadima mimed frantically bailing out water with her hands.

'Is no food. Is no water. Boat is rocking, rocking. People sick on us.'

I climbed into the box and we huddled together. 'They were in the middle of the ocean. There were no other boats around to help them. They couldn't see any land. They were lost. Then it got dark. Everyone was very, very frightened.'

Then Nadima stood up and helped me climb out of the box.

'In morning boat land. Where are we? Everyone asking. Somebody say Italy. Nobody know.' She shrugged. 'We walk on road. Walk. Walk. Walk. Then we see sign!'

I held up a poster we'd made of a 'Give Way' sign.

'Is English! We in UK! We so happy we all cry!'

I rolled up the poster and said, 'Then the police arrived and took them all to a hostel. Nadima's parents were frightened they would be sent back. But after a while they were told they could stay.'

Then Nadima held up the photo I'd taken of her family. They were standing outside their new house. She took a deep breath and said, 'This is my family. This is our home. We all are learning English. We are safe and we very happy to be here. Thank you.'

'The end,' I said.

There was absolute silence when we'd finished. 7R just stared at us. Nobody clapped. Nobody said anything. I think they were gobsmacked.

I looked over at Mrs P and was shocked to see she was crying. Really crying. She was trying hard not to show it, by doing a lot of sniffing and blinking hard, but she wasn't winning.

Finally she wiped her eyes on the sleeve of her kaftan and managed to pull herself together. 'Well, Nadima,' she said, and speaking *slowly* to Nadima (for once) she said, 'We are all very happy that you are here, and that you got here safely. Thank you for telling us your story. Well done, both of you.' And she started clapping. So the rest of 7R started clapping too . . . and they carried on clapping while Nadima and I grinned at each other and did a high five before we sat down. Then Kara started whooping and cheering, which gave the rest of the class the excuse to go totally over the top. Mrs P didn't even try to calm them down.

I looked at Nadima. Her eyes shone and I thought she was going to explode with pride.

50
Friends

At break, everyone gathered round Nad and me like chocolate chips on a double-chocolate-chip cookie. It was a boiling hot day, so we all sat in the shade of a tree in the back field.

'It must have been a terrifying journey,' Lily said to Nadima.

'Yes. Was terrifying.' Nadima nodded.

'You must be incredibly brave,' said Chloe.

'I don't think I could have done it,' agreed Elly. 'I don't even like going on the ferry!'

Nadima shrugged. 'Is no choice.' Then she added thoughtfully, 'Rasha and Sami brave. They very little.'

'Sami's only about two,' I told everyone. Suddenly I had an image of him in the boat. A tiny, frightened little boy, with his long dark lashes plastered on his chubby wet cheeks and his eyes wide with fear.

'Did you think you were going to die?' asked Kara. And I knew she wasn't being melodramatic. She really meant it.

'Yes,' said Nadima simply.

'Kind of glad you didn't!' I said, putting my arm round Nadima.

She grinned at me.

'Me too!' she said.

The others laughed.

'It was a good idea to do your story, Nadima,' said Lily.

'Was Jaz idea,' replied Nadima.

'Well, I thought it was *fantastic*, Jaz!' said Kara. 'Really clever and . . . and . . .' She tailed off, like she couldn't find the right word.

I shrugged. 'I just thought it was important to tell everyone.'

'Yes, "*important*". That's *exactly* the right word,' said Kara. 'And I *loved* the way you did it – especially tearing up the photos. It was really *effective* – so *dramatic*.'

'Did you see Mrs P? I thought she was going to burst into tears!' said Chloe.

'I thought *I* was going to burst into tears!' said Kara, flapping her hands melodramatically in front of her eyes, as if she was welling up again just thinking about it.

Then we all swept Nadima up into a group hug, and I thought *she* was going to burst into tears!

51
🍴 Happy Eid! 🍴

That evening after school Nadima texted me:

🍴 **Friday 6.30**
Is Eid. Can you come?

I texted back:

YES!

So on Friday I went back to Nadima's after school. They took me to this Kurdish restaurant, run by some people they had made friends with.

It was really small, and it was *amazing*! I'd never been anywhere like it. Nadima said it was just like the restaurants back in Syria. But *everything* was Kurdish! The music . . . the food . . . even the menu.

There weren't any chairs. We all sat on big colourful cushions around a large low table. Huge lanterns hung from the ceiling, spilling coloured light and making everything look magical. Brass candleholders threw flickering patterns around the room. The scent of the food drifting out from the kitchens, and from other people's meals, was warm and spicy and *soooo* tempting! I remembered the first meal Nadima's mum had ever cooked me.

Sami had clambered onto Nadima's lap while they all looked at the menu and decided what to order. They were speaking in Kurdish and Sami must have said something funny because they all laughed, and Nadima's dad ruffled his hair. Her mum shot them such a look of love it made my throat go all tight.

Watching her family together, celebrating and laughing, looking so happy, you'd never guess what they'd been through. Not just back home in Syria but also on the frightening journey they'd made getting here. Not to mention having to start a new life all over again, in a country where they didn't know anyone, or even speak the language. It made me realise how strong they were. All of them. It made me proud of Nadima, and proud to be her friend.

Nadima turned to me and handed me the menu. Then, pointing at some of the dishes, she added, 'We get this, and this, and this. We all share. You choose too! What want?'

Actually, there was a bit of a problem with the menu. I couldn't read it. Not because it was in Kurdish – there was an English bit as well – but because it was written in a fancy font and, as you know, I really, really, struggle to untangle those. Why don't people think? Lots of dyslexics can't read curly-whirly letters. It drives me nuts. Anyhow, I didn't want to admit in front of Nadima's family that I couldn't read the menu. So I pretended to look at it for a while, and I picked something at random.

Nadima gave me a funny look. 'Not lamb? You love lamb!'

'Um . . . I thought I'd try something else.' I shot her a look and hoped she wasn't going to make a fuss.

She looked at the menu. 'Is funny writing,' she frowned. 'Is very hard to read. We choose together, OK?'

I grinned at her. 'Fine!'

Once we'd ordered, Nadima's mum fished in her handbag and handed Nadima a present. Nadima promptly handed it to me.

'Is for you. Is present for Eid,' she said. I was mega-embarrassed. I hadn't realised presents for Eid were a thing, and I didn't have anything for any of them. Her family were all looking at me and smiling expectantly. So I undid the paper and took out the present. It was a bracelet.

'Nadima make for you!' said Rasha shyly.

'You like it?' asked Nadima.

'Yes, I love it!' I said, holding out my arm for her to tie it onto me. 'Thank you!'

It was made from plaited blue and silver threads (my favourite colours) with letter beads strung onto it. The beads were simple white squares with black letters. Apart from the first letter, which was a capital letter, the rest were little letters. She must have chosen them specially so it was dead easy for me to read. It said:

N a d i m a

'Is Kurdish friendship bracelet,' she said, 'It says "friend".'

'No, it doesn't!' I laughed, giving her a friendly shove. 'It says "Nadima"!'

'Ah, but name "Nadima" *means* "friend",' she said, smiling that smile which lights her whole face up.

'Actually, the name "Nadima" means "*Best* Friend" to me. "*Best Friend Forever*"!' I said, throwing my arms round her in a huge hug.

I'll never forget the day I met Nadima.

From the moment we swapped chunks of chocolate and Turkish Delight, I knew, I just knew, we were going to be best friends. And I also know we always will be. Don't ask me how. I just know.

Acknowledgements

Do You Speak Chocolate? was inspired by friendship and powered by chocolate.

My most sincere thanks to:

Naomi Colthurst – for instantly liking the idea from the moment I pitched it to her and commissioning the book.
'For instant happiness – just add chocolate.'

Georgia Murray (my editor) – for helping guide Jaz and Nadima through the perils and pitfalls of friendship, and the perils and pratfalls of narrative chaos.
'Amidst the chaos, there is always chocolate.'

Talya Baker (the copy editor) – for stoically, no, heroically, correcting all my multiple mistakes.
'*Keep Calm and Eat Chocolate.*'

Gaia Banks (my agent) – for never losing confidence in me, or the book, and for being thoroughly wonderful.
'*Never underestimate the power of chocolate.*'

Kate Forrester (illustrator) – for a front cover that's even more delicious than melted chocolate.
'*Chocolate and books are all you need.*'

JW – for telling me to write the book in the first person, and TB – for reminding me to write the pictures.
'*Chocolate is like good advice: it makes everything better.*'

My fabulous kids – for putting up with having a cranky, distracted writer for a mother and for not raiding my secret chocolate supply – even though they know where it is.
'*Life happens – chocolate helps.*'

The two girls, who appeared in the BBC Schools documentary about friendship, and whose names I unfortunately don't know – for inspiring the book, with their profound determination to become friends, despite not speaking a word of each other's language, and proving that: 'The language of friendship is not words but meanings.' (Henry David Thoreau)
'The language of friendship is chocolate.'

Finally, my mates – for being there for me, always. Girls, it would be impossible to thank you enough in one small acknowledgement – it would take a whole book. Which is why I'm dedicating this one to you.
'There is nothing better than a friend – unless it's a friend with chocolate.' (Linda Grayson)

CAS LESTER spent many years having a fabulous time, and a great deal of fun, working in children's television drama with CBBC. She developed and executive produced lots of programmes including JACKANORY, MUDDLE EARTH, THE MAGICIAN OF SAMARKAND, BIG KIDS and THE STORY OF TRACY BEAKER.

Now Cas writes books for children (the HARVEY DREW series; WILFRED THE UNWISE; NIXIE THE BAD, BAD FAIRY). As Patron of Reading at a local primary school, Cas is currently setting up and helping run the school library. She loves working with children and especially doing school visits. She has four children, a daft dog called Bramble and she lives in Oxfordshire. To contact her about a school visit go to her website: www.cas.lester.com.
Follow Cas on Twitter: @thecasinthecat

Jaz and Nad's 'Chocolate Turkish Delight'

Hiya!
Here's how to make our *inspired* sweets!

<u>You need:</u>
A box of Turkish delight (We would give you the
recipe for Nad's mum's Turkish Delight – but it's
top secret! Sorry!)
Large bar of milk chocolate

A microwave-proof bowl
A microwave
A big plastic or wooden spoon or spatula
A skewer or fork (one for each person making the
sweets)
A big plate

<u>This is what you need to do:</u>
1. Open the box of Turkish delight and maybe try a
   couple of pieces! Just to make sure they taste all
   right!
2. Break the milk chocolate into chunks and put them
   in the microwave-proof bowl.
3. Melt the chocolate in the microwave on 'high'.
   Give it 30 seconds at a time and then stir it.
   Repeat until the chocolate is melted. (You don't
   want to overdo it because it will go gritty.)
4. Stick chunks of Turkish delight onto either a
   skewer or a fork and dunk them in the melted

276

chocolate. You might want to tap some of the
icing sugar off them
first – to help the chocolate to stick. Then put
them on the large plate to cool. You will probably
get covered in chocolate – but who cares!

Top tip
They'll cool quicker in the fridge – but they taste
better if they're at room temperature

Eat and enjoy!

Love from
Jaz and Nad x

Nad's Mum's Fabulous Fattoush

Here's our favourite salad recipe!
This makes enough for two people as a side dish.

For the dressing you need:
About 1/3 of a mug of olive oil
The juice and the grated zest of one lemon (or you
can just use lemon juice)
½ teaspoon of chopped garlic
About 2 tablespoons of sumac (This is a sour-tasting
spice. You can get it in a jar from most
supermarkets. Nad says it's better if you can get it,
but if you can't then just make it without.) Btw
DON'T put all 2 tablespoons in at once! Add a bit
at a time, then taste it and add more if you like it.
Salt and pepper

You will also need:
A mug
A knife, a grater and a lemon squeezer (if you're
using a whole lemon)
A tablespoon and a teaspoon
A bowl
A whisk

To make the dressing, just bung everything in the
bowl and whisk it!

<u>For the salad:</u>

Well, it's sort of up to you what you like in your
    salad. But we like:

½ a cucumber (peeled and cut it into chunks)

10 cherry tomatoes (cut in half)

½ a yellow pepper (or a red or orange one) cut into
    chunks

3 spring onions (or half of a red onion) sliced up
    small

¼ of a big crunchy lettuce – chopped up

4 radishes sliced thinly (you can leave these out if
    you don't like them)

1 pitta bread (brown or white) – tear this into bits

You can also add a small handful of chopped fresh
    herbs – either parsley or mint or both.

<u>You'll also need:</u>

A peeler and a kitchen knife

A chopping board

A big serving bowl

Chop up all the salad stuff, put it all in the big serving
    bowl and mix it up. Then add as much of the
    dressing as you like! (Nad's mum says you can keep
    the rest of the dressing in a plastic tub in the fridge
    for about a week.)

Hope you like this as much as we do!
Nad and Jaz x

Jaz's Awesome Tuna Pasta Bake

This is supposed to be enough for a family of four –
but I have to make *loads* more to feed my
ridonkulously sporty, hungry big brothers!

You need:
500g dried pasta
A handful of frozen peas (or sweetcorn if, like Dan,
   you don't like anything green)
250g Cheddar cheese
2 tins of tuna
300ml carton of cream (fresh or long life)
Salt and pepper

A saucepan
A microwave-proof bowl
A microwave!
A grater
A plate
A tin-opener
A big ovenproof dish
A sieve
A big spoon
An oven!

This is what you need to do:
1. Put the oven on to heat up to 180°C/gas mark 4.
2. Cook the pasta in boiling water in the saucepan
   for about 2 *minutes less* than it says on the packet.

While it's cooking:
   a. cook the peas or sweetcorn in the microwave for 3 minutes
   b. grate the cheese onto the plate
   c. drain the tuna and put it into the big ovenproof dish.

3. When the pasta is done, strain it in the sieve and put it into the dish with the tuna. Add the peas or sweetcorn, pour the cream over and add half of the cheese and some salt and pepper. Give it a good stir. Then sprinkle the rest of the cheese over the top.

4. By now the oven should be at the right temperature. Bung the dish in the oven and cook it for about 15 to 20 minutes till it goes a bit brown on top.

5. BE VERY CAREFUL when you put the dish in the oven and EVEN MORE CAREFUL when you take it out again. ALWAYS USE OVEN GLOVES and remember to put the hot dish onto a mat or a trivet or something so it doesn't burn anything.

You might want to make a salad to go with it, but in the winter, The Brothers like it with baked beans.
(Me too!)

It's dead yummy – promise!
Love from
Jaz x

Piccadilly
PRESS

Thank you for choosing a Piccadilly Press book.

If you would like to know more about our authors, our books or if you'd just like to know what we're up to, you can find us online.

www.piccadillypress.co.uk

You can also find us on:

We hope to see you soon!